"I'd hit the lowest point in my life. I had become two things that I'd said I'd never become. I was a junkie and a prostitute."

Jackie left home looking for trouble— and found much more than she could handle. Hers is the story of a teenager's search for genuine love—perhaps a search you can identify with. Find out how Jackie finally met Someone who could meet her deepest needs.

BY *John Benton*

Carmen
Teenage Runaway
Crazy Mary
Cindy
Patti
Suzie
Marji
Lori
Sherri
Marji and the Kidnap Plot
Julie
Debbie
Lefty
Vicki
Jackie

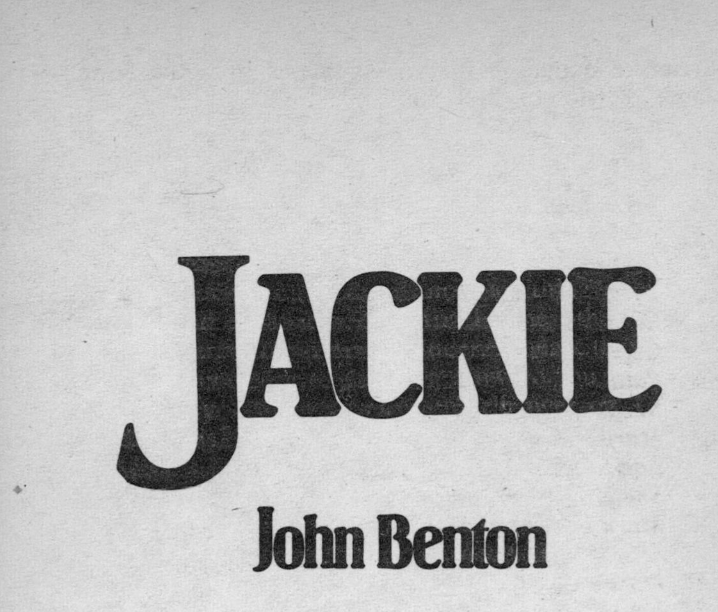

JACKIE

John Benton

Fleming H. Revell Company
Old Tappan, New Jersey

Scripture quotation in this volume is from the King James Version of the Bible.

ISBN:0-8007-8406-5
A New Hope Book

Printed in the United States of America
This is an original New Hope Book, published by New Hope Books, a division of Fleming H. Revell Company, Old Tappan, New Jersey.

TO
my special friend
Bev Zechar
who really knows how
to bring Christ's love
to many hurting girls

1

Over the blare of the late-afternoon TV reruns I could hear Mom cursing a blue streak in her bedroom. Now what was the matter?

"Jackie!" she yelled.

I could tell by the way she called my name that I was in trouble. Even though I was almost seventeen, she still treated me like her little baby, and—

"Jackie, have you seen my pearl necklace?"

Oh, no! I had no idea she planned to wear that to dinner with Dad tonight!

"Come help me find it, Jackie!"

Find it? I knew exactly where it was—down inside my bra! I needed a little extra cash, and this seemed like the perfect way to get it. She saved that necklace for very special occasions, and I figured it would be a long time before she missed it.

"Jackie, you get in here, right now. And shut that TV off!"

I wasn't really engrossed in the TV anyway, so I flipped it off and ambled back to her bedroom.

"What's the matter?" I asked as nonchalantly as I could.

"It's that pearl necklace your father gave me for our twenty-fifth anniversary. I was sure I had put it right here in the jewelry box the last time I wore it. Now I can't find it anywhere!"

"Oh, Mom, you are always forgetting where you put things. I've heard Dad tell you that a thousand times. I'm sure it's around here somewhere. Let me help you look."

I walked over and opened the jewelry box. Of course, I knew it wasn't there, but I rummaged through her other costume jewelry. I remember thinking, *There isn't much else of value here.*

Walking over to her closet I remarked, "Maybe you left it in your coat pocket the last time you wore it."

"Are you kidding?" she responded. "I wouldn't leave expensive pearls in my coat pocket! That would be stupid! There is only one place I would have put them—in my jewelry box. That's where I always put them. But they're not there now!"

My heart started beating like crazy, and I felt as though I were about to faint. If I passed out, Mom would check my heart—and probably find her pearls. I couldn't let that happen.

My head kept feeling lighter and lighter. Maybe if I just bent over. . . . No way! I couldn't do that! Those pearls might pop out of my bra!

"I've got to get a drink of water," I told her. "I feel faint."

"What's the matter?" Mom asked, turning her concern from the search to me. "You look awfully white."

I had to think up an excuse. "It's my period," I told her.

That usually stopped any questions. When Mom turned and started digging through her drawers, I knew it had worked.

Out in the kitchen I grabbed a glass and took a long drink. Then I sat in a chair and put my head between my legs. After a few minutes, my head began to clear. I drew a deep breath; I felt so much better.

I could hear Mom still rummaging around in her bedroom. I couldn't afford the finger of suspicion being turned on me, so I figured I'd better get back in there.

"Oh, I'm so upset," Mom told me when I walked back in. "Are you sure you haven't seen my pearls anywhere?"

I wished she'd stop asking questions like that! I felt my head getting lighter again.

I went over and started poking through her drawers, suddenly realizing they were as messy as mine!

"Charles!" Mom yelled.

No answer. That wasn't surprising. Dad was in the shower. He couldn't hear anything or anyone when he was in the shower.

"Charles! Do you hear me?"

Still no answer.

She banged on the bathroom door as though she were trying to wake the dead. "Charles! Charles!" she yelled again.

I heard him turn the water off and slide the door open. "What do you want?" he yelled.

"Oh, I'm so upset!" she yelled back. "I can't find my pearl necklace anywhere. Have you seen it?"

I could hear Dad laughing. Then he yelled back, "Haven't I always said you were just like your mother? Neither of you can ever remember where you've put anything. If you'd put it where—"

"That's not funny!" Mom interrupted angrily. "And you leave my mother out of this. This is that expensive pearl necklace you gave me, and I'm sure I put it in my jewelry box."

Dad yelled back that he'd be out in a minute to find it for her. He usually could. But he wasn't going to find her necklace this time. That is, he wasn't if I could carry this off!

In a moment he walked out of the bathroom with his pants on but no shirt. "Now what's the matter?" he asked.

"It's that pearl necklace you gave me four years ago. I could swear I put it in my jewelry box, but it's not there."

"Well, it's bound to be around here somewhere," Dad replied. "When was the last time you wore it?"

"A couple of months ago when you took me out to dinner. When we got home, the first thing I did was put it away—in the jewelry box, as I always do."

As Dad walked toward the jewelry box, I knew I'd better get into the act.

"Are you sure you had it on then?" I asked. "I don't remember you wearing it."

"Yes, I know I wore it," she said. "I remember at dinner looking around and noticing that none of the other women had on pearls. I worried that maybe I was out of style."

"Well, maybe the strand broke," I said. "A lot of restaurants have carpeted floors now, and you wouldn't have heard—"

"Impossible!" Mom interrupted. "I asked the jeweler about that when I got the pearls. He said it couldn't happen because they were double-knotted. So it would be absolutely impossible for them to break that way."

Now maybe I was asking too many questions! They were the wrong ones, and I was getting the wrong answers. So I decided to try another approach—something closer to the truth.

"Maybe someone stole them," I said.

Mom's mouth flew open. She covered her face in horror and said, "Oh, no! I hadn't even thought about that! But who would do something like that?"

Dad had ceased his searching and was looking at me very suspiciously. I should have kept my mouth shut.

"Hey, listen, you two," I said. "You know this neighborhood as well as I do. A bunch of these kids around here are on drugs, and they're busting into houses left and right. Don't you remember that the Burris's house was broken into a couple of weeks ago?"

"Say, that's right," Dad responded. "Maybe they got in here, too, and we're just realizing that things are missing!"

"Oh, no!" Mom said again. "They wouldn't do that, would they?"

"Mother, Mother. Welcome to the twentieth century," I said. "You'd better believe they would. Most of the kids I know at school are on drugs, and they'll do anything to support their habits!"

I held my breath. Would this throw them off course?

"Well," Mom said, resuming her search, "I don't believe anyone stole my pearls. Why would they take just the pearls?"

How was I going to answer that? "I agree, Mom. I'm sure you've simply misplaced them."

"I really don't know," Dad said thoughtfully. "We'd better start locking things up better. And, Nancy, I think you ought to replace that jewelry box with one you can lock."

"That wouldn't do any good," she replied. "Then they would just steal the whole box. The only thing we can do is get a safe."

"Hey! Great idea!" I chimed in. "Then I can keep my valuables in there, too. I just know that one of these days our house is going to get robbed."

Mom was methodically going through her drawers. But I was pretty well convinced that she didn't suspect me. Still, I needed to keep up my act, so I knelt down and started feeling under the bed.

"What are you doing down there?" Mom asked.

"Looking for your pearls. Maybe you took them off

and put them on your nightstand and then accidentally knocked them off. It's surprising what gets kicked under the bed."

Running my hand back and forth, I hit something, but it was too big to be a necklace. I grabbed it and pulled it out. Dad's watch!

He hadn't had it too long, and I knew he had paid a lot for it because Mom had fussed about it at the time. I thought I could get at least fifty dollars for it—and one hundred dollars for the pearls. That would make one-hundred-fifty dollars! I could buy enough drugs to keep me going for a good while!

But Dad was smart. I didn't want to arouse his suspicion and blow the whole thing. I could lie to Mom—that was easy. But Dad, now that was a different matter. And if he found out, he'd beat me.

But if I gave him the watch now, that would throw all suspicion off me about the necklace. So I yelled, "Dad! Look what I found!"

They both spun around to see as I held the watch high in the air.

"Jackie, where did you find that?" he asked in pleasant surprise.

"Right here under the bed. I told you, it's amazing, the things that get kicked under a bed!"

He walked over and took the watch from my outstretched hand. "You're a lifesaver," he said gratefully. "I've missed this for two days now, but I didn't want to say anything to your mother. After all the bad times I've given her about losing things, she never would have let me hear the end of this!"

He slipped the watch over his wrist and gave me a big smile.

I got up off the floor, congratulating myself on my cleverness. Sure, I'd given up fifty dollars. But I knew that now they were off my case!

I walked back into the living room and flipped on the TV to get the early-evening news. My parents were going out to dinner again, and I had told them I would be staying home. But I had plans to take off, too. I'd buy my drugs and then have a big party. But I had to make it look like I'd be home all evening.

Suddenly I became aware that my dad had followed me into the room and was saying, "Jackie, turn that TV down. I want to talk to you a minute." He settled onto the sofa.

I obeyed. I knew there'd be big trouble if I crossed him. He was a real tyrant.

"Jackie, now I don't want you to think I'm accusing you or anything," he started in. "But while we were back there in the bedroom, you seemed to be awfully nervous. Is something wrong?"

Just as I thought. I could never fool Dad. But maybe if I told a big enough lie, it would throw him off the track.

"Dad," I said, "you might as well know the truth. I'm pregnant."

"You're what?" he exploded, jumping to his feet.

"Pregnant. I'm going to have a baby."

He stood there with his mouth open. "Jackie, I can't believe this. I mean, I just can't believe it. Are you sure?"

"Well, I think so," I replied. "Do you remember a couple of months ago when I went to baby-sit for the Overtons? Well, when Mr. Overton was bringing me home. . . ."

I carefully studied Dad's expression. "That's why I'm so nervous," I said.

Dad dropped back onto the sofa, perspiring profusely. His fists were clenched so hard his knuckles had turned white.

"Well, we'll settle this right now," he shouted. "No

middle-aged Romeo is going to. . . ."

He started for the phone, and I broke out laughing. He whirled around in surprise. "Dad, it was all a joke! I'm not pregnant!"

His look of anger turned to shock, then disbelief, and finally a smile as he realized what had happened. "Oh, for crying out loud, Jackie. You really had me going on that one, didn't you!" Then he joined my laughter.

Mom came out of the bedroom demanding, "I'm glad somebody can find something to laugh about. I still haven't found my pearls. Now what's so funny?"

"Jackie just told me she's pregnant," Dad answered.

"Pregnant?" Mom yelled. "Are you sure?"

"Yes, Mom. I'm four months along."

Dad almost doubled over with laughter. But Mom was getting so upset she looked as though she were going to faint!

"That's not funny!" she screamed. "What are our neighbors going to say?"

Dad was laughing so hard he was holding his side. "Nancy, it's just a joke," he finally explained.

"A joke?" Mom echoed. "You've got a weird sense of humor if you think that's funny!" She stomped back to the bedroom.

Well, maybe Mom was in no mood for a joke. But it had worked with Dad!

But he sat down again and said, "Now, Jackie, since we have taken care of your pregnancy, would you please tell me what is really bothering you?"

So my bombshell hadn't worked. Now what?

Thinking quickly, I replied, "Dad, I don't want to hurt your feelings, but I'm seriously thinking about getting my own apartment."

He was on his feet again. "Getting your own apartment?" he repeated incredulously. "Jackie, you're only sixteen, and—"

"Almost seventeen," I interrupted.

"Jackie, Jackie. This is absolutely stupid."

"No it's not, Dad. Mary Ann, my friend, has her own apartment. Maybe I could move in with her."

"Mary Ann Andrews?"

I nodded.

"Don't you know about her, Jackie? From what I hear, she has parties going on all the time at her place. It's a real den of iniquity. No way will I ever give you permission to live with her. Why, one of these days the cops will raid her apartment and bust a whole bunch of kids for drugs. So you can just get out of your mind any idea about moving in with her!"

I guess I just blew it. I really didn't want an apartment. But I had started the line, so I had to stay with it.

"But Dad, I guess I'm just restless or something. School's getting to be such a bore. You know what I mean?"

He nodded. "Jackie, you're just going through a phase," he told me. "All teenagers go through it. It's called restlessness. Some people call it stirring up the nest. It's nature's way of preparing you to have a home of your own. It's why lots of kids drop out of school when they're juniors and seniors. But if, as I told your brother, Clarence, they'll just hold on a little while. . . ."

"You mean Clarence wanted to drop out of school?"

"Yes. He was seventeen and a senior, and he wanted to drop out and join the Marines. I found out that Clarence just wanted to be a man. I tried to tell him that you don't become a man overnight or by joining the Marines. That seemed to satisfy him."

I never knew much about Clarence's youth. He was ten years older than me. In fact, Mom used to joke with me that when I came along, I was an accident. My folks didn't want any more children after Clarence, but I came anyway. I always resented it when she talked that way—even though she said she was joking. It sure doesn't help your self-image to feel you were not wanted!

"Jackie," Dad said, "something deeper is bothering you. Do you want to tell me about it?"

Before I could start in on another story, he looked straight into my eyes and asked, "Jackie, do you know where your mother's pearls are?"

I hadn't expected that question!

I almost raised my hand to pull out the pearls and hand them to him. But something kept screaming in the back of my mind not to do it. I had to have those pearls to get money for drugs to get high. And getting high felt so good.

"Dad," I said, "you can't possibly know how deeply you have hurt me by asking that question. You're accusing me of taking them, aren't you?"

He dropped his head and looked at his hands. "Jackie, I'm not saying anything like that. I'm just asking if you know where they are."

"Dad, you're not asking a question; you're accusing me. You think I'm a thief, don't you? You probably think I'm the one who's been breaking into houses in the neighborhood. Dad, I just can't believe you feel that way about me. I just can't believe it."

"Now, Jackie, I didn't say all that. You stop putting words in my mouth. I just asked you a simple question—one that you can very easily answer with a yes or a no."

"Dad, if I were a thief, would I have given you back your watch?" I asked. "Of course not! That was an easy setup. You had no idea where you'd lost it."

Was I glad now that I had given him his watch back! This should throw him completely off my case!

"Dad, look at me," I continued. "Look straight into my eyes."

He slowly raised his head and turned toward me. I knew he was feeling guilty, so now I was going to sock it to him. "Dad, I want to tell you this straight. I have no idea where Mom's pearls are."

He quickly shifted his gaze back to the floor. I knew I had him. And it surprised me to know I could lie to him so easily.

He slowly got up and started back to the bedroom. "Jackie," he said brokenly, "please forgive me. I have no reason to accuse you of anything."

My heart leaped. "Oh, come on, Dad," I said. "It's okay. I know how you feel. No hard feelings. Okay?"

He just nodded and continued on to the bedroom to finish getting ready. I was so relieved I wanted to jump up and down and squeal for joy. But that would bring demands for explanations. So I simply turned my attention back to the TV.

The news was almost over when the two of them came to tell me good-bye. "We might take in a movie, too," Dad said, "and be out kind of late. Are you sure you're okay here by yourself?"

"Dad, stop treating me like a little baby," I said, laughing. "Of course I'll be okay. I'll keep the doors locked, and I won't let anyone in. Besides, if I'm old enough to get my own apartment—"

"What's this about an apartment?" Mom interrupted.

"Nothing," I replied. "I had said something to Dad about it, but I've decided it would be foolish. No way am I going to start getting drunk and shooting drugs. When people get apartments, they become junkies and prostitutes."

Dad smiled. I knew he was thinking he had talked me out of that idea. That was okay. Maybe this would keep their minds off the pearls.

"My goodness, Jackie," Mom said. "I'm glad to see

you're finally getting some sense in your head. I'm proud of you!"

If they only knew the truth! But I didn't care. All I thought about was getting high, and as soon as they got out of there, I was on my way!

When they went out, I turned off the TV so I could be sure to hear the car start up and then back out. From the front window I watched the taillights of the car until they turned a corner and were gone. Finally!

I pulled out the pearls and studied them. They did look beautiful—and expensive. I knew Dad had paid five hundred dollars for them about four years ago. They were probably worth even more now. I pushed them back into my bra for safekeeping, hurried upstairs to my bedroom to get my purse, bounded back down, and hit the sidewalk running. I quickly covered the two blocks to the subway. Living in the Bay Ridge section of Brooklyn had its problems, but at least we had good transportation. Brooklyn seemed to be crumbling, but Bay Ridge maintained its character. There were a lot of nice homes in our neighborhood, and I was fortunate to live in one of them. Dad made a good living selling cars.

I had just started down the stairs at the subway station when it hit me. Where was I going? Obviously to a pawnshop, but which one? I should have looked one up in the phone book before I left home. Maybe I should have called to be sure they were open in the evenings. Oh, well; I could find someone who'd tell me.

I pushed my money through to the man in the subway-token booth, and he pushed back a token. "Mister," I said, "do you know where there's a hockshop in Manhattan?"

He stared. "You don't look like a thief," he said. "What in the world are you doing with hot merchandise?"

I grabbed my token and spun around. Was this guy a cop? How did he know I had stolen those pearls?

I was pretty sure there would be some pawnshops around Thirty-fourth Street. Maybe somebody there could give me directions.

In a few minutes I was on the subway train. I made a couple of transfers, and before long emerged at Thirty-fourth Street. People were walking every which way. Whom did I dare stop and ask about a pawnshop? Would they know which ones were open?

Then I noticed a cop standing on the corner. He surely would know about hockshops. But was it dangerous to ask a cop?

I decided it wasn't any more dangerous to ask a cop than to stop a stranger. So I walked over and asked, "Mister, do you know where there's a pawnshop open around here this time of evening?"

He looked me up and down. I knew what he was going to ask, so I beat him to it. "Hey, don't get me wrong, I'm no thief. I'm learning to play the guitar, and a friend told me you can get some good deals on guitars at hockshops."

He smiled. Good! "I didn't think you looked like a thief," he said. "And your friend is right about the guitars. They've got lots of them. But half of them have been stolen."

"Stolen?" I asked in mock horror. "Man, I don't want to buy hot merchandise. Maybe they'd sell me one that wasn't stolen?"

He laughed. "If you ask the owners, they'll tell you that none of them are stolen. But that's their problem."

"Is there one around here?"

He pointed. "Go on down to Seventh Avenue. Turn right and walk two blocks. There's a couple of them down on Thirty-second and Seventh."

I followed his directions and soon saw the sign RANDOLPH'S PAWNSHOP. I was relieved to see the lights on inside.

When I opened the door and the man behind the counter looked at me quizzically, a horrible thought occurred to me. Suppose this was a decoy policeman! Maybe that's why that cop had sent me down there!

2

The worry about whether the guy was a decoy cop almost made me turn around and leave. But then I thought of the money—and the drugs. I had to go through with this.

Walking nervously toward the counter, I noticed that the guy standing there was short and fat and sloppy. I hated being in there alone with him.

"Hey, kid, what do you want?" he called, eyeing me up and down.

Talk about nervous; that really did it. I had never stolen anything before. I had never been to a pawnshop before. And I had no idea what kind of people—

"Tell me what you want or get out!" the guy snarled.

His belligerence made my knees turn to jelly, and I steadied myself against the counter. I set my purse down and snapped it open to pull out the necklace. Then it hit me! The pearls were still in my bra! Now what was I going to do? I started to reach up toward my blouse. The old man watched my every move. When he saw where my hand was headed, he sneered, "Hey, hey! No problem! Let me help you!" He reached toward my blouse, but I slapped his hand in disgust. "What do you take me for?" I shouted. "Keep your filthy hands away from me!"

He grabbed my blouse and pulled me over the

counter toward him until his face was about two inches from mine. "You little creep!" he shouted. "Nobody gets smart with me, and that includes you, kid. I once had a smart-aleck kid like you at home. Every time she mouthed off, I did one thing. I slapped her silly. I can't stand little girls with big mouths who have no respect for their elders!"

Because I was so nervous, a lot of saliva had formed in my mouth. Before I thought about what I was doing, I spit. And at that distance I couldn't miss! It splattered across his mouth!

He spluttered and swore, and I jerked away. Out of the corner of my eye I saw his other hand coming toward me. I ducked, and his fist whooshed through clear air. It was a good thing that counter was between us. But I felt a button pop as I went sprawling backwards onto the floor.

I jumped up and headed for the door. But he screamed, "Stop, kid! Or it's all over!"

I stopped because he had a gun pointed right at me!

Instinctively I raised both hands. "Okay, mister, you can put the gun away. I'm sorry. I mean, real sorry."

He kept the gun trained on me as he moved out from behind the counter. "I ought to blow your brains out," he sputtered, still wiping his face with his free hand. "Never in my life has anyone spit in my face and gotten away with it!"

"And never has anyone grabbed my blouse and tried to get fresh with me!" I retorted. "I ought to call the cops on you, buster."

The guy laughed. "Great idea, kid. Great idea! I happen to work for the police department; so go ahead—call them!"

"What do you mean, you work for the police department? It looks to me as though you run a filthy little hockshop. I don't think a cop would set foot in this place."

The old man laughed again. "Don't you know, kid, that a lot of stolen merchandise is brought in here? I take it, of course; but as soon as the customer walks out the door, I call the cops. The cops and I work together."

His sinister laugh terrified me. If he only knew I had stolen pearls in my bra. Maybe he did know! I'd better straighten things out with him.

"Mister, I'm sorry," I said. "I just needed some money and thought maybe I could work a deal with you. That's all."

"What kind of deal?" He asked. "Do you have hot merchandise?"

Was this a trap? He had just gotten through telling me he worked with the police. I knew I'd better get out of there as fast as possible.

"Look, mister, you and I got off on the wrong foot," I said. "I've changed my mind about the deal. But I did something bad to you. So why don't you just spit in my face to even the score? Then I'll get out."

Had I really said what I just heard? How could I possibly. . . .

I must have said it because he stepped toward me, his gun still aimed at me. I could see his throat moving up and down. I squinched my eyes tight. I heard him spit and felt it strike my forehead and run down my cheek. Every muscle in my body tensed; my stomach tightened into knots; my hands formed into claws. I wanted to leap at that filthy old man and scratch his eyes out. But I wouldn't even give him the satisfaction of seeing me wipe it off.

I opened my eyes slightly—just in time to see his throat moving again. I tried to duck, but the spittle smacked right on my nose!

"May I get my purse?" I asked softly. "I want to leave now."

He lowered the gun. I retrieved my purse from the counter and headed for the door. Out on the sidewalk, away from where he could see me, I took my handkerchief out of my purse and wiped the spittle off my face. While my purse was open, I reached into my bra, got the pearls, and stuffed them and the filthy handkerchief back in. And then I burst into tears.

I guess it was an emotional reaction to the horrible thing I had just been through. People stared. Some even stopped. But no one said a word or offered to help me. It reinforced my feelings that no one really cared about what happened to me.

I felt better when I got the tears out of my system. The experience had made me determined to do one thing: I wasn't going to let anything stop me from hocking that necklace—not even a creepy owner who spit in my face.

Down the street I spotted another sign: BERGMAN'S PAWNSHOP. The lights were on inside, so I headed in that direction, wondering if Mr. Bergman would be mean and ornery like Randolph.

When I walked inside, I saw two people talking with a man behind the counter. I couldn't believe it, but the guy behind the counter looked enough like Randolph to be his twin brother! Would he act like him, too?

Since I knew these owners cooperated with the police, I decided I'd better check all three of these people out before I said why I was there. So while they talked, I wandered over and started looking at a case of jewelry. But I also kept my ears open.

The man behind the counter was saying, "Listen, Lance, as I told you, there's absolutely no way I can take those diamond rings."

"Oh, come on, Mr. Bergman," Lance begged. "You

can do it one more time. I'll give you a good deal. These diamonds are worth over one thousand dollars. You know that as well as I do."

"I'm not disputing your price," Mr. Bergman replied. "It's just that I can't afford to buy hot merchandise."

Lance jumped back in feigned horror. "Listen, Bergman, don't you accuse me of selling hot merchandise!"

"Okay, okay, I'll level with you two," Mr. Bergman said. "The last time I bought diamonds from you, as soon as you walked out that door, two plainclothes detectives came in and demanded to know what you two were doing in here. I tried to cover for you and say I'd never seen you before. Well, when they said they knew you had been in here four or five times, I figured they had had the place staked out. I got a little nervous about them shutting down my business, so I showed them the diamonds. And what did those two detectives do? They said they had to take them for evidence. They said I'd get them back—someday. But in the meantime I've got all that money tied up, and there's no way I can get to it. I don't know whether to take the diamonds you have now and give you nothing, or wait until those cops bring the other ones back."

The two customers started to laugh. "Bergman, you're a sucker!" Lance said. "Did those detectives show you their badges?"

"Of course they did."

Lance doubled over. "Bergman, you were set up. Those two weren't detectives. They were imposters. I know. They've done the same thing at a pawnshop across town where I've been doing business. You just lost a couple of good diamonds to some con men!"

"What?" Mr. Bergman said in surprise. "You have to be kidding!"

"No, I'm not kidding. I'd be willing to bet ten thousand dollars you'll never see those rings again!"

Mr. Bergman let loose with an oath that burned my ears. "If those two ever come in here again," he said, "I'll kill them. In fact, I think I'll call the cops and blow the whistle on them. Nobody's going to rip me off like that and—"

"Hey, Bergman, cool it," Lance interrupted. "Do you know anything about those two? One guy's name is Angel. The other is called Devil. And they're mean dudes. I mean, they are mean!"

"How do you know?"

"Well, over on Twenty-ninth Street there's a hockshop that's all boarded up. You know which one I mean?"

Mr. Bergman nodded. "Sure. Cy Obert's place."

"Well, Cy Obert isn't there anymore," Lance said.

"What do you mean by that?"

"Cy called the cops on Angel and Devil. They found out about it and paid him a little visit. That's why his store is boarded up—he's dead!"

I wasn't paying much attention to the jewelry in the case as I heard that story unfold. I wondered what on earth I was getting into. Maybe I'd better take the pearl necklace home and forget this whole hockshop routine. It was a lot rougher than I had figured on. But I had to have money if I was going to get high.

"Listen, I don't care what happened to Cy Obert," Mr. Bergman said. "And I don't care what happens to you guys. But there's one thing for sure. I just can't afford to buy any more diamonds from you guys. I don't know you that well. And if I buy them, a couple of cops will probably come in and demand them for evidence again. I don't know if you're telling me the truth or not."

Lance spun around in disgust. That's when he first noticed that I had entered the pawnshop. He sidled up to me, and I backed up a little. He was big and awesome. I sure didn't want to get into any hassle with him.

"Little girl," he started in, "don't be afraid. I'll protect you, just like your big daddy."

This Lance was perceptive. I knew I was scared to death over this situation, but I didn't think it showed all that much.

He gently put his hand on my arm. "I'll tell you what, little girl," he said, sounding for all the world like a supersalesman on TV. "I'm going to give you an opportunity to make some easy money. I'm going to give you this beautiful diamond—free! Then you hock it. Bergman will give you five hundred dollars for it. After you hock it, you give your big daddy the five hundred dollars, and I'll give you fifty dollars for your trouble."

I glanced at Mr. Bergman. He was shaking his head vigorously.

"Lance, get out of here before I call the cops!" he shouted. "There's no way I'm going to buy that diamond—either from you or from that little girl. Besides, you'd better quit picking on her. For all you know she may be a decoy cop!"

Lance laughed at the preposterousness of that comment. Then he got serious and punched his finger toward Mr. Bergman. "I'm going to give you tonight to sleep on this, Bergman," he said. "Tomorrow morning Bradley and I are coming back. I think you'd better do business with us, or we might do an Angel and Devil job on you. Then there'll be another hockshop all boarded up!"

He turned on his heel, and he and Bradley stormed out. Mr. Bergman just stood there, watching. Neither of us said a word.

As the door slammed behind those two, I slowly walked over and put my purse on the counter. This time I had those pearls where they should be. Without a word I pulled them out and handed them to him.

He studied them carefully. "Are these hot?" he asked.

I slammed my hand down on the glass counter so hard that it rattled the glass. "Listen, mister," I screamed, "let's start off on the right foot. I'm no thief. I'm no girl from the street. I got these from my boyfriend on my eighteenth birthday. He comes from a wealthy family. Well, after he gave me the pearls, I discovered he was using them as a way to get something more. You know what I mean? I was so mad I broke up with him. But I kept the pearls."

Mr. Bergman stepped back a little. "Okay, I believe you! I believe you! You've got enough temper there to handle anybody!"

He reached under the counter and pulled out a light. He studied the pearls, turning them over and over.

"How much do you want?"

"One hundred dollars."

"One hundred dollars?" he said in surprise. "Oh, I couldn't do that. I'd really be sticking my neck out to loan you fifty dollars on these."

I knew they were worth a lot. Was Bergman trying to take advantage of me because I was young—and a girl?

"Wait a minute!" I exploded. "Those pearls cost five hundred dollars. You—"

"How do you know they cost five hundred dollars?" he interrupted.

I bit my tongue just as I was about to say that was how much my dad had paid for them for my mother. "Well, when my boyfriend and I were having this big argument, he yelled that he had paid five hundred dollars for the pearls, and he thought he ought to get some kind of return on his investment. I believed he paid that for them."

"Yes, they are good pearls," Mr. Bergman said. "Very good ones, in fact."

"Okay, then it's one hundred or no deal," I told him.

"Okay," he said. He pulled out a drawer and handed

me a form to fill out my name and address. I was so relieved about getting the one hundred dollars for the pearls that I didn't even think about what I was doing. I simply wrote my real name and address down. I found out later that that was one of the most stupid things I had ever done.

Mr. Bergman grabbed the form and studied me.

"Kid, are you telling me the truth?"

"Of course. My name is Jackie Marshall. I live in Bay Ridge."

"I don't believe you."

"Oh, for crying out loud. What do you want me to do? Do you want me to call my mommy and daddy so you can ask their permission?"

"It's not that. I just don't like to deal with young kids. How old are you anyway?"

"I told you, I'm eighteen."

"Do you have any identification?"

"I have a social-security card."

"Driver's license?"

"Nope. Dad won't let me drive. Says the insurance is too high."

"Well," Mr. Bergman said, "I don't like to deal with teenagers. And I don't think I could ever sell those pearls. I can only give you fifty bucks."

Before he knew what was happening I had snatched the necklace out of his hands and tossed it back into my purse.

"Okay, Mr. Bergman," I shouted, "if that's the way you do business, I don't want anything to do with you. I'll take my pearls elsewhere."

I whirled and headed for the door. But before I could get to it, it opened. And there in the door stood one of the biggest, burliest policemen I had ever seen.

You can believe I stopped dead in my tracks as my heart started racing.

"How's business, Mr. Bergman?" the cop asked pleasantly.

"Not too good," he answered. "Seems as though everybody has an exaggerated opinion of what their stuff is worth. You know what I mean?"

The cop looked over at me. Why did Mr. Bergman have to say that, anyway?

"I just wanted to stop by for a minute," the cop said. "I'm working on a case. Maybe you can help me."

"Hank, you know me," Mr. Bergman said. "I've cooperated with you in the past, and I'll do it again."

"Well," the cop said, "last night there was a break-in out at Kennedy Airport. There were some expensive—and I mean extremely expensive—pearls from Japan stolen."

I stiffened. Suppose that cop demanded that I open my purse, and found those pearls. There was no way I could convince him they were my mother's! If I said that, he'd call my parents. Either way I'd get busted. I gripped my purse tighter.

"I'm sure whoever broke in to get them is going to hit the streets to try to peddle them," the cop went on. "So if someone comes in here with pearls, can you give me a call?"

My heart just about stopped. Did I dare try to make a break through the door? If I did, would Mr. Bergman yell for the cop to stop me? Then it would really be all over!

"Hank, you know you can count on me," Mr. Bergman replied. "If anybody tries to peddle any pearls, you'll be the first one I call."

I had my back toward Mr. Bergman, facing the policeman. I just knew that dirty old pawnshop owner was pointing his finger right at me the whole time. Any moment that cop would step up and slap his handcuffs on me and haul me away to jail.

Instead, the policeman slowly turned and opened the door. "See you, Mr. Bergman," he called. And then he was gone.

I sighed with relief. That was too close!

As I reached for the door handle, Mr. Bergman called, "Well, young lady, I guess you can thank me for saving you from doing twenty years in the slammer."

"Yes, I guess you could say that," I answered, trembling. "I'd better be going."

"Just a minute, young lady. I think you owe me a favor, don't you?"

I whirled around. Don't tell me he was a dirty old man.

"What do you mean, I owe you a favor?"

"Listen, little spitfire, it's not what you think," he replied. "I'm a happily married man, so I'm not talking about that kind of favor. I'll loan you fifty bucks on those pearls. It'll cost you sixty bucks to get them back. Now that's the favor I'm talking about. You take a little less for them because I didn't squeal on you."

I walked back to the counter. I guessed I did owe the old guy something, and fifty dollars was better than nothing.

He reached into his pocket, pulled out a wad of bills, and laid two twenties and a ten on the counter.

I opened my purse, pulled out the pearls, and started to lay them on the counter. Before I could, he snatched them out of sight.

I jumped back, startled. He sensed my fear and said, "Little girl, just cool it, will you? How many more of these do you have stashed away? I'll take all you can bring me."

Oh, no! He really thought I was the one who had knocked off that shipment of Japanese pearls at Kennedy. I'd never been out to Kennedy Airport, so I sure didn't know where they would store pearls.

"Mr. Bergman, if you think for one minute that I'm the one that cop was talking about, you've got another thing coming. No way would I get involved in something like that."

"Oh, come on, kid. I've been in this business for forty-five years. These big boys are smart. When they knock off a shipment, they hire kids like you to go to the hockshops. I know that." He looked right into my eyes as he said it.

"You've lied to me ever since you came in that door," he accused. "Now come on. Level with me. How many more pearls like those can you bring me?"

He was busy inspecting the pearls again, and he wasn't expecting what I did next. I snatched them away. And I wasn't expecting what he did next. He reached under the counter and pulled a gun!

"Listen, a deal is a deal," he said. "Now give me back those pearls."

"Okay, okay!" I responded. "Take the stupid pearls. But there is no way I am going to get involved in any shipment of pearls from Japan. Absolutely no way."

How could I convince him? I glanced at them.

"Here, take a look at the clasp," I said as the idea struck me. I pushed it right into his line of vision. He lowered the gun.

"If these were hot ones just in from Japan, that clasp wouldn't be worn that way. These are not new pearls."

"Okay, kid, I see what you mean."

I gently dropped the strand into Mr. Bergman's waiting hand, scooped the fifty dollars off the counter, stuffed it into my purse, and was halfway to the door when he yelled, "Hey, wait a minute! You forgot something!"

I whirled around. What in the world was it this time?

"You forgot your claim check. You have to have this in order to get those pearls back."

I walked back to get it and stuffed it into my purse, too. That was another stupid thing to do, because that claim check was going to nail me to the wall sooner than I realized!

3

To this day, I don't really know why I did it. But when I went into the subway, rather than going back to Bay Ridge, I headed up toward Times Square, the drug capital of the world.

I got off at Forty-second Street and began looking for a pusher. That wasn't a problem; they were everywhere. I had been taking drugs for almost two years, so I could readily recognize pushers.

I saw a man leaning up against a wall. I walked up to him and asked, "Are you dirty?"

He laughed. "Hey," he said, "what do you think I am?"

His answer irritated me. "Listen, punk; who do you think I am—a plainclothes detective dressed like a girl?"

The guy looked me up and down while I studied him. After all, he might be a cop.

I guess he was very much aware I was looking him over because he asked, "Do you like what you see?"

So that was it. He thought I was a prostitute. I would show him! I moved up close, threw my arms around him, and murmured, "I've never seen such a hunk of man in all my life. You are the answer to my every dream!"

All the while, I was rubbing my hands up and down

his back and then along his sides. Next, I dropped to my knees and felt his legs. No guns.

He looked down at me, puzzled, and asked, "What on earth are you doing down there? Get up and tell me your game."

I got up, stepped a few paces back, and laughed. "Mister, I'm no prostitute. I'm no decoy, either. But I had to find out about you. You're no cop, either."

"Of course I'm no cop," he answered, laughing. "And I know you're not, either. While you had your arms around me, I touched your purse. You're not carrying a gun."

This guy was smart. But why was he out here on the street? He didn't look like a junkie. And he hadn't really given me a straight answer about whether or not he was a pusher.

I asked if he knew anyone around who was dirty, thinking that if he were a pusher, he'd let me know, rather than miss a sale.

"Look across the street," he told me, nodding in the general direction. "See that guy looking down Forty-second toward Times Square? He's got drugs."

As I turned to walk away, he called, "Stay cool, kid; he could be a cop."

I spun around. "Now why did you have to say that? You're not kidding me, are you?"

"Hey, listen, all I know is that while I was standing here, I watched a couple of people cop drugs from the guy. But I've never seen him before. Wise up, kid. Maybe he's a cop. You know, cops are all over this place."

I knew he was right. But I also knew I really had no choice. I wanted drugs, so I had to trust my luck.

I waited for the light to change, crossed over, walked right up to the man, and asked, "Have you got two bags?"

He studied me carefully, then looked across the street. Had he been watching me check out the guy over there? Were the two of them working together? Were they both cops?

"Yes," he said. "I have two bags. Forty bucks."

I opened my purse and pulled out two twenties. The man fumbled inside his pocket and pulled out two bags. My money changed hands for his dope. It seemed too simple. I hoped he had good stuff.

"Hey, baby, who do you work for?" the pusher asked.

I stared at him blankly. I knew what he was driving at, but I didn't want to dignify it with an answer. Then he said it plainly: "Do you have a pimp?"

"Listen, mister," I exploded, "I don't know who you are, and you don't know me. You're just lucky I'm not an undercover cop. I'd slap handcuffs on you and haul you away for a life sentence! So get something straight. I'm no prostitute, and I'll never be one of those filthy things!"

The very thought of prostitution had always disgusted me. I couldn't imagine any girl selling her body that way. It was absolutely degrading.

The pusher laughed. "You have a lot of fire in you, don't you, baby? Maybe you're not interested now. But when you get uptight and need some money for dope, come see me!"

I whirled and stomped back across the street. The man I had been talking to before met me at the crosswalk. "Hey, baby," he said, "I noticed that you scored. I hope that guy has good stuff."

"I was hoping the same thing," I replied. "I heard that now and then you can get a hot shot around here—nothing but rat poison."

"Listen, kid," he said. "I don't know how much you know about drugs. But before you get off, make sure you taste it. Just put a little on the tip of your tongue, and you'll know what it is before you jam it into your veins."

"Hey, how come you know so much about drugs?"

The guy laughed. "I've been around. I've been around."

I should have gone home, at that point. But it was late, and I was afraid my folks might be home already. Besides, I wanted to get off right now. Why wait? There was only one problem. In my rush to get away, I had left my set of works stashed in our basement.

I studied the man again. I had a hunch he was street-wise. "Hey, do you know where I can get a set of works?" I asked him.

"Sure. I have a set in my apartment."

He didn't look like a junkie; he wasn't strung out. He was even well dressed. Was he trying to set me up?

"Okay," I said, "so you have a set of works in your apartment. How much is it going to cost me to use them?"

"One bag."

"One bag?" I repeated in surprise. "Man, that's twenty bucks! I'm not about to pay twenty bucks to use a set of works."

"Fine with me. Forget it, then."

Could I trust this guy? Was he a pimp, trying to get me hooked on drugs so he could push me out into the streets to sell my body so he could collect the profits?

"How do I know you're not a pimp?" I asked.

He stiffened. "Hey, little girl, I've been called a lot of names, but that is one I won't let anybody call me. I'm not a pimp, and I never will be a pimp. I've got two sisters at home. I used to have three. But one of them came here to Forty-second Street, and a pimp picked her up. She worked for that guy for six months, and then she tried to get rid of him. She got rid of him, all right! That dirty, filthy, good-for-nothing pimp killed her! I would have killed that pimp, but somebody beat me to it. He's dead; my sister's dead. But one thing remains: I can't stand pimps. So don't you ever call me a pimp!"

I stared at the pavement, feeling so ashamed. "Hey, mister, I am sorry. I mean, I had no idea. I was just looking out for myself. You never know who you may meet around here."

"I know what you mean, little girl. There are all kinds of pimps. I'm surprised you haven't been picked up yet. What are you doing out here—besides buying drugs?"

Drugs! That reminded me of his works. His proposition was looking more and more inviting.

"Okay, mister, I'll tell you what. Let's go to your apartment, and I'll give you a bag so I can use your works. Then I'll tell you a little more about myself."

He smiled. "This way. My apartment is on Forty-sixth Street."

Apartment. That word made me nervous. What had I gotten myself into now? I had heard stories about what sometimes happens to young girls who go to men's apartments. They are raped—maybe murdered. And these terrible things are done by the people you would least suspect.

So as we walked, my heart beat faster and faster. I was sure I had reason to be scared!

I wondered if I should run to get away. But really, he wasn't forcing me to accompany him. And something magnetic kept me by his side. I still hadn't figured him out.

We turned onto Forty-sixth and came to a run-down apartment house. Now I was really worried, but I followed him in. As we walked up to the second floor, I decided I'd better find out a little more about him before he got me into his apartment.

"Hey," I said, "after all our conversation, I still don't know your name."

"My name? John Wayne."

"John Wayne? Like the actor from Hollywood?"

He nodded. "What's yours?"

"Marilyn Monroe."

"You mean like that beautiful blonde?"

I nodded. I'd given him a taste of his own medicine. Then I asked, "Okay, what's your real name?"

"Michael Burke."

"Okay, Michael, let's see some identification."

He pulled out his wallet, flipped it open, and pushed his driver's license almost against my nose. Yes, that was his name.

"And what's your name, Marilyn Monroe?"

"Jackie Marshall."

"Identification?"

I pulled out my wallet and pushed my social-security card up to his nose.

"You have a cute name," he said with a grin. "And you're a cute kid. I think I like you."

What did he mean by that? Was he going to try to seduce me? I'd better be careful!

As he was fumbling for his keys in front of his apartment door, I said, "Michael, I've been trying to figure you out. You apparently aren't a pusher. You said you're not a pimp. What are you, anyway?"

"I sell hot dogs on Forty-eighth and Avenue of the Americas. Have you ever seen me down there?"

"You sell hot dogs? I don't believe it!"

He had the door opened by that time, and motioned me inside as he laughed and said, "No, I'm not a hot-dog salesman. But I am a salesman."

The apartment sure didn't have any class. It wasn't really messy, but it sure wasn't neat, either. The upholstery on the sofa was worn almost threadbare, and the other furniture looked like rejects from a secondhand store. If he was a salesman, it sure didn't look as though he was a very successful one!

He closed the door and locked it—in four different places. Every time he slammed one of those bolts shut, I shuddered. If this guy was up to no good, there was no way I was going to get out of there. The window was slightly open, but we were on the second floor. If I tried to jump, I'd probably kill myself.

Michael immediately headed for the bathroom—to get his set of works, I assumed. I picked a spot on the sofa that didn't look too grubby, opened my purse, and pulled out the two bags. In a moment, Michael was back with his works. He sat next to me and began to set up. He had everything I needed.

"Here, let me check one of those bags for you," he said. He pulled a bag from the coffee table, unraveled it, touched his tongue to the stuff, and then exclaimed excitedly, "Hey, man, you have good stuff here!"

I got the works ready. "Do you want me to drill you?" Michael asked.

"Sure, why not?" I replied. It was always hard for me to hit the main vein. Then, in a stroke of caution, I asked, "Do you know what you're doing?"

He smiled. "Watch me, baby; watch me!"

I handed him the needle. He rubbed the veins in my arm, right in the armpit. Then he hit the needle. First try, and he had it.

How come this guy knew so much about drugs? How come he knew so much about needles? And how come he wasn't a junkie?

"You sure know your way around with a needle," I told him.

"Yes," he said. "I'm a doctor."

"A doctor? You don't look like one, but you sure act like one. You hit my vein the first time."

He didn't respond. Instead, he pushed the plunger. The drugs hit my veins, and I went sky high. I mean, I really scored.

Michael calmly pulled out the needle, and I slowly leaned back on the sofa. I was going to stay here awhile and enjoy this.

He grabbed the other bag, put it in his pocket, and disappeared as he took his set of works back to the bathroom. Was he going in there to drill himself?

No way. He was back too soon for that. He had the drugs; he had the works. But he wasn't going to use them! I couldn't understand that, so I said, "Come on, Michael, tell me what you really do."

"Okay, Jackie, I'll level with you. I'm a pusher."

"You're a what?" I asked in surprise.

"A pusher."

"Hey, if you're a pusher, how come you didn't sell me drugs?"

"I'm too smart for that, Jackie. I only have certain customers. I have good drugs, and they know it. I never pick up somebody walking the streets. That's a good way to get your head busted—either by the cops or some wild junkie."

Was he putting me on again? He sure didn't fit the image of a pusher. And why would a pusher—who made oodles of money—live in a dump like this?

"Michael, I thought pushers had fancy cars and lived in plush apartments."

"Sure, everybody thinks that," Michael responded. "Why, when the undercover cops start looking for the pushers, they look for the guys in the big cars and expensive apartments. They don't waste their time looking for guys in run-down apartments. Sure, I've got lots of money. But I don't put it into fancy cars or plush apartments. That might give me away. Instead, I keep a low visibility level. I've been pushing for two years now and have never been busted."

If he was telling me the truth—and I had no reason to disbelieve him—he sure seemed smart. Yet I wondered how long it would be before the cops noticed him. Eventually the cops caught the pushers—at least, that's what I read in the newspapers.

I sat there nodding, enjoying my high. And although I half expected Michael to make an approach, he didn't even touch me.

Some time later we heard a loud bang on the apartment door—not really a knock; it sounded as though somebody threw something at the door. Michael and I both jumped up, startled, and looked at each other. "What do you suppose that was?" he asked.

"I don't know. Were you expecting a customer?"

Michael had a terrified look on his face as he said, "No, I wasn't expecting anyone. I never let my customers come here. I meet them on the street. You don't think we were followed, do you?"

"Not me," I responded. "Nobody knows I'm here—not even my parents."

When I said that, I realized how vulnerable a position I had put myself in!

Michael tiptoed over to the door and peered through the eyepiece into the hall. Then he turned around and whispered, "There's nobody there."

"Maybe it's some kids playing games."

"At two in the morning? Jackie, are you sure you're on the level? This isn't a setup, is it?"

"Michael, for crying out loud, I'm telling you the truth. Unless," I paused as I said it, "unless that guy I bought my drugs from was a decoy cop. He might have followed us!"

That idea hadn't even entered my mind until this moment. We hadn't tried to hide where we were going when we came up here. It hadn't even occurred to me that this could happen.

Michael moved across the room, opened a drawer,

and pulled out a gun, which he tucked inside his belt.

"What are you doing that for?" I asked nervously—knowing full well what he was doing it for.

"I smell a rat," he said. "And a person needs to be ready for rats!"

At that moment the telephone rang, and both of us jumped.

"Don't answer it!" Michael ordered. "They may be checking to see if I'm here."

"It's your phone," I replied, as it kept ringing and ringing.

Then I said, "Maybe you ought to answer it to let them know you are here. Maybe somebody just pounded on the door to see if anyone is home. Maybe they plan to break in, but they're checking the place out. If you answer the phone, they'll know you're here and won't bother you."

"Hey, Jackie, that's smart. Maybe you're right."

He walked over and gingerly picked up the receiver. "Hello?"

He held the receiver for a moment, then slowly put it back in the cradle. "They hung up," he announced.

"Michael, what do you think is happening? Do you think someone is out to get you?"

"I don't know," he responded. "There are all kinds of possibilities. As you say, it could be a couple of junkies trying to break into the apartment. It could be under-cover cops. And it could even be other pushers. This is a ruthless business, Jackie. Pushers will steal from another pusher—especially when they know he just got a big shipment in."

"You just got a big shipment?" I asked nervously.

"No. I'm sort of down right now."

Pacing back and forth he said, not really to me, "What in the world am I going to do? If it's the cops, I'd better get away. But if it's junkies, I'm going to wait them out. If they come through that door, I'll kill them. My .45 automatic is dependable. And I'm a crack shot."

My high was wearing off, and I was growing more terrified by the minute. How in the world had I ever gotten myself into this mess? All I had wanted to do was buy some drugs. Now here I was, about to be part of a drug bust or maybe a witness to murder! I'd better get out of this place as fast as I could.

"I think I'd better leave, Michael," I announced, with a lot more bravery than I felt. "My folks will be worried."

He grabbed my arm. "Jackie, I can't let you walk out that door. There may be a couple of ruthless pushers out there in that hallway, and they'll stop at nothing! They'd kidnap you to get to me!"

I put on a front. "I'm not afraid of a couple of pushers. I've been around. And I'm getting out of here."

"Jackie," he said, letting go of my arm. "I just thought of something. Can I trust you?"

"Of course. Why?"

"Well, like I told you, I'm really low on drugs right now. I've got only twenty bags or so left. I think I can trust you, so let me give you all of them. You stuff them into your bra and your boots and walk out of here. I'll meet you at Forty-second and Eighth and get my bags back. In fact, I'll give you five bags for helping me."

He seemed eager for my cooperation. But could I really trust him? Suppose I walked out there, and the cops were waiting? They'd find drugs on me and bust me; Michael would go free! I guess that's what he was figuring, too.

Michael must have been reading my thoughts. "Jackie, when you go out, let's pretend you just came up here to shack up with me. I know that idea is distasteful to you—you're not a prostitute. But we'll just act it out when we open the door. That way, if it's pushers out there, they won't touch you. And if it's the cops, they're going to have to catch you in the act. So they won't touch you, either. What do you say?"

I wasn't delighted about the situation. But five free bags of dope sounded like a great idea. And I had a suspicion that Michael had good dope!

"Okay," I told him, "it's a deal."

He hurried back into his bedroom and brought out a bunch of bags, which I began to stuff into my bra and my boots. They sure felt uncomfortable. Would I look suspicious?

I grabbed my purse and walked stiffly toward the door. Michael unlatched it. This time I shuddered every time one of those bolts unlatched!

As he opened the door, he threw his arms around me and kissed me passionately. Then he said loudly, "Okay, baby, I'll see you tomorrow night. And fifty dollars will be waiting for you then, too!"

I put on a big act myself. "Oh, thank you, thank you. You can count on me to be back!"

Even while I was saying those words, I kept wondering about what was waiting for me down that hall. Michael shut the door. I could hear him hitting all those locks. He was safe. But what about me?

At the stairway I peered down into the darkness. Dare I descend? Could I get to the street safely? Maybe I should go back in and stay until morning. Then I thought of five free bags. I'd go through with the deal.

I hurried down the stairs. Nothing happened. I breathed easier when I got out on Forty-sixth Street. Then I remembered. It was past 2:00 A.M. I would be easy prey for a mugger!

Halfway down the block toward Eighth Avenue, I had

this strange sensation I was being followed. I spun around. Just as I did, two big bruisers ducked into a doorway.

Who were they? Why did they jump back? Were they really after me? Why?

4

I quickened my pace and got to Forty-second and Eighth okay. There was no sign of those two creepy characters who seemed to be following me. Maybe I was just imagining things.

But now I was faced with another problem. Michael didn't say how soon he would meet me. And what if someone broke into his apartment and killed him?

I knew I was loaded with dope. I could sell it, shoot it, or do whatever I wanted to do—Michael would never know the difference. Or at least he'd never find me!

Well, I waited and waited and waited some more. Still no Michael. I couldn't risk just standing around there forever. What if a cop got suspicious? If he searched me, I'd be put away for a long, long time.

When it seemed obvious to me that Michael wasn't coming soon, I decided to head on home. So I walked to the subway station, took the stairs down, and changed my money for a token. I pushed the token into the slot and walked through the turnstile to that familiar *click, click.* But I hadn't gone but a few steps inside when I heard *click, click; click, click.* I quickly turned, and coming through the turnstile were two thugs. They looked about the size of the two I thought I had seen following me when I came out of Michael's apartment. Were they the same ones? Or was it still my imagination working overtime?

I started down the platform, and I heard them following. I stopped. They stopped. I turned toward them. As soon as my eyes met theirs, they looked the other way.

I walked a little farther, and I heard them walking. I stopped again. They stopped. Then I whirled around. Both of them were staring right at me, but this time they didn't turn away.

Who were these two characters, anyway? Did they suspect I was carrying drugs? Had Michael hired them to keep on eye on me?

I spotted a nearby bench and went over and sat down to wait for the subway train. They moved in closer. Nobody else was in sight. If only somebody else would show up, I'd feel a little safer. Why didn't that train get here? This seemed like a nightmare!

Finally I heard other footsteps. I looked and saw a policeman walking toward me. Then I glanced back and noticed the two thugs edging away from me a little. Now I knew for sure they were up to no good. I'd better tell the cop.

When I stood up to walk over to where the cop was, I remembered a problem. I was loaded with drugs. Suppose those two guys knew I was carrying drugs. If I complained to the cop about them and he talked to them, they'd tell him about me. What a mess! There was no way I could tell the cop those two thugs were after me!

The cop walked over and asked, "Are you from New York City?"

"Yes," I responded. "I live in the Bay Ridge section of Brooklyn. Why?"

"My goodness, young lady, I would have thought you were smarter than that," he said. "A pretty little girl like you has no business being out late at night like this, especially here in the subway. Don't you know that your chances of making it home are almost nil?"

"I collect tickets at the Rialto Theater," I lied. "I just got off work after a late show. I think I'll be all right."

I knew I wasn't going to be all right. Those two thugs still stood waiting in the background. Both of them had their hands in their pockets. Did they have guns?

"Officer," I went on, "if it makes you feel any better, when I left work tonight, I told the manager I wasn't coming back. I think you're right. It is too dangerous working these late hours. So tomorrow I'm going to look for a job near my home."

"That's a smart idea, young lady. Here's hoping you make it home tonight."

I wished he hadn't said that. I was scared enough as it was. Now I was absolutely terrified.

The subway train stopped, and I got on. I hoped the police officer would get on, too, but he just stood there. Then at the last minute, before the doors slammed shut, those two thugs jumped on.

I slid into a seat in the almost-empty car. The two thugs walked toward me and sat on either side of me.

I assessed my chances. Down at the end of the car were two old guys with their heads bowed, probably sleeping off a drunk. They sure couldn't help me.

I wanted to jump up and run, but I knew these guys meant business.

"Look here," one of them ordered.

I glanced in his direction as he pulled his hand from his pocket, revealing all I needed to see of a gun.

As we pulled into the Thirty-fourth Street station, I hoped a cop would get on. But one of the guys said, "Okay, young lady, we're getting off here—and you're going with us. Do as we say, and you'll live. Try any smart moves, and you'll be dead!"

The way he said it, I knew he'd have no qualms about carrying out that threat.

They stood up and pulled me to my feet between them, so I didn't have much choice. I wondered whether Michael had put these guys up to following me, and I was going to get it because they thought I was trying to steal his drugs. Or maybe they had already killed Michael for his drugs, and learned that I had all his drugs on me. Either way it was a no-win situation for me.

As we walked up to Thirty-fourth Street, I said, "Come on, you guys; level with me. What's the deal? I'm just a young girl who lives in Bay Ridge and wants to go home."

"Shut up!" one of them ordered. "When we want you to talk, we'll tell you. In the meantime, don't even think one word, or it's all over for you. Understand?"

I nodded. I sure wasn't going to give them any trouble.

We stood at the curb, waiting for a taxi. They finally hailed one and pushed me into the backseat between them. "West Sixth just off Avenue of the Americas," one of them told the driver.

That meant they were taking me down to the Village. Why? Would they take me down an alley and put a bullet through my head? Or were they going to rape me?

Maybe if I made a deal and gave them all the dope, they'd let me go. So I leaned over to the one who seemed to be the leader and whispered. "Okay, I'll make a deal with you. I've got some bags of dope here in my bra. I'll give those bags to you. All of them."

A sinister smile flashed across his face. "You say you have a bunch of dope?" he repeated. "Is that what you're trying to tell me?"

I nodded as I said, "Yes, that's it, mister. I've got good dope—and you can have it all."

"You'd better believe I can have it all—and whatever else I want!" Then he lowered his voice and almost spit the words at me: "And I mean, we're going to take all of it!"

They must have known I had dope on me. But how?

I reached up to unbutton my blouse, but they grabbed my arms and pulled them down. "No funny business!" the leader ordered. "Keep your hands in your lap. You pull a switchblade, and it's all over."

"Listen, I don't have any switchblade. I don't have any gun. All I've got are these bags of dope."

"Keep your mouth shut!" the leader ordered again.

I did. In a few moments, the cab pulled to the curb on Sixth Street, and we got out. One of them paid the driver, and he took off with his wheels squealing. Then the two thugs grabbed me, one on each arm, and led me down the street.

I kept my eyes open for numbers. If I got out of this alive, I was planning to tell the cops.

We walked two more blocks—I guess to get away from the place where the driver let us out, so it would be harder to trace them. Then as we walked by an alley, one guy gripped my arm hard. "Okay, kid, we're walking down that alley. You let out a scream, and I'm slamming a bullet through your brain!"

I couldn't see anything down that darkened alley, but the smell almost nauseated me. We stumbled along over garbage until they slammed me up against a wall.

"Okay, little girl, let's have the dope," one guy said. When I didn't respond that second, he grabbed my blouse and started pulling. Bags of heroin spilled to the ground.

The guy slapped me hard across the face, yelling, "Listen, when I tell you to move, do it quickly! You hear me?"

I nodded. One guy was picking up the bags on the

ground. I started pulling the remaining bags out of my bra and handed them to the leader. I wasn't worried about saving any dope. I was worried now about saving my life!

"Okay, do you have any more on you?"

"Yes, sir, I do. I have some in my boots."

I slid down to pull off my boots. One of them yelled, "Hey! Wait a minute! Don't you dare reach your hand inside those boots!"

They were still skittish about the possibility of my having a hidden gun or knife. So I said, "Okay, you pull them off."

So there I was, sitting on the ground in that stinking alley, and those two guys grabbed my boots—both at the same time. They yanked so hard I thought my feet would pull away from my ankles! As soon as the boots came off, more dope spilled out on the ground. They stuffed it greedily into their pockets and demanded, "Do you have any more any other place?"

I realized if they searched me it could get embarrassing and humiliating. So I quickly said, "Listen, I swear that's all I have." I patted the midsection of my body. "See? There's nothing here."

I instinctively reached out and grabbed one guy's hand, pushed it against my hip, and ran it along my side.

I tried to see his eyes in the darkness of the alley. I sure hoped I was convincing enough.

He did a little patting of his own and then announced, "Okay, but you're lucky, kid. The last time Michael Burke used a carrier, he resisted us, so we had to knock him off. Good thing you went along with us."

So they knew Michael. But how did they know I had the drugs?

"Do you guys work for Michael?" I asked as innocently as I could.

One of them laughed derisively. "That Michael Burke

is a creep," one of them said. "He's trying to muscle in on our business. We're not going to put up with nonsense like that. I would advise you to stay as far away from him as you can. One of these days he is going to end up dead in the Hudson River. And other people might get hurt, too. Know what I mean?"

He didn't have to say any more. I never wanted to see Michael Burke again.

"You're really lucky that we didn't have to kill you," he went on. "Now my buddy and me, we're going to walk out of this alley. You stay in here for ten minutes. So help me, if you try to call the cops, it'll be all over for you. My advice, little girl, is for you to get as far out of this city as you can and never come back. You're too young to be messing around in this dangerous business."

I knew he was right. And that's where I planned to head right now—home—if I could make it.

The two guys turned and walked back toward the street. I stood where they had told me to stand, scarcely daring to breathe.

They disappeared, and I waited a few minutes. I tried to do the best I could with my blouse—two buttons had been popped off tonight. It wasn't one of my best nights!

I got to the street, and they were nowhere around. I'd been down to the Village before, so I knew where I was, but I never had had an experience like tonight's! I was stunned. What I had been through was absolutely preposterous.

This time when I got on the subway, I was in such a daze that I didn't notice whether or not anyone else was around.

I finally got home. Carefully unlocking the front door, I tiptoed upstairs to my bedroom. I dropped onto my bed, physically and emotionally exhausted from what I had just been through. I trembled as I thought of what could have happened. I was lucky to still be alive!

The next thing I knew, my mother was shaking me. "Jackie! Wake up! You must have overslept again. You'll be late for school!"

I blinked my eyes and stared at her. School? I didn't feel like going to school—not after last night. But I hurriedly dressed and headed for the kitchen.

Dad had already finished breakfast and was drinking his coffee and reading the sports page. I grabbed a box of cereal, poured some into a bowl, added milk and sugar, and sat down.

All this time I was aware that Dad was watching me over his paper, but he hadn't said a word.

I toyed with the spoon in my cereal. Nothing looked appetizing.

"What's the matter?" Dad demanded. "Not hungry?"

"No," I answered.

"You seemed to come home awfully late last night. Where were you?"

I sure couldn't tell him where I was. The whole thing was so preposterous that he wouldn't believe it, anyway. But mostly I couldn't let him find out about my drug habit.

"Oh, I just went over to a girl friend's house," I lied. "We got involved in a real late movie on TV. I figured you wouldn't mind. You told me you'd probably be out late, anyway."

"Jackie, I hate to keep bringing up the same subject, but I still can't find my pearl necklace," Mom said. "You didn't wear it somewhere, did you?"

I almost choked on the bite of cereal I had in my mouth. I'd almost forgotten about the necklace. Was that just last night? It seemed like ages ago!

"Me, wear your necklace?" I managed. "You know I don't wear necklaces."

"Are you sure you don't know where that necklace

is?" Dad insisted. "Are you telling me that you haven't seen it?"

The tone of his voice really irritated me. This was worse than being grilled by the cops. Angrily I pushed my bowl of cereal back, splashing milk onto the table. "For crying out loud," I yelled, "what's the matter with you two, anyway? Are you accusing me of stealing Mom's necklace? What are you trying to do to me? Don't you trust me?" With that, I jumped up.

Mom came over and put her hand on my arm. "Now Jackie, just calm down," she said. "I'm sure I just misplaced it."

But Dad yelled, "You sit down right this minute, young lady. That's no way to act toward your mother and father. Now I asked a question, and I expect a straight answer!"

I stood there glaring. "Sit down!" he ordered again.

I wanted to run to the serenity of my bedroom. But maybe if I obeyed, I'd be in less trouble. So I slid onto the chair.

"Now, young lady," Dad started in, "it seems as though you are out later more often these days. I mean, it seems that every other night you're gone. And you're coming in terribly late."

"What do you want me to do?" I snapped. "Take a little slip with me and get it signed everywhere I go? Is that what you want?"

Dad shook his fork at me. "Young lady, you're going to start showing some respect for me!"

"Don't point that fork at me," I countered. "It makes me nervous!"

He dropped his fork and grabbed my arm, yelling, "Don't you dare talk to me that way!"

I jumped up, jerked my arm away, and shouted, "You get your filthy hands off me!"

That was just like lighting a fuse. I ran out of the kitchen. I heard Dad push his chair back and start after me, and I heard Mom say, "Now, Charles, take it easy. She's just upset over something."

I knew I had to get out of the house before the situation exploded—even if it meant going to school. So I ran upstairs, grabbed my books from the dresser, and headed down the stairs toward the door. Oh, no! There stood Dad, blocking my way.

As I reached for the doorknob, he said, "I hope you have more respect for your teachers than you do for your parents! And I hope you get some sense in your head!"

I didn't respond. I was boiling inside. As I ran down the porch steps and along the street, I almost decided to keep running instead of going to school. But I figured I'd better cool it.

My school was six blocks away. Just as I walked in, I reached for my purse, and realized I'd forgotten to bring it. Oh, well. I could borrow some money from one of the kids for lunch. And I could get along without any additional makeup.

All day long I couldn't keep my mind off drugs. I had to think of another way to get money so I could get high. Maybe I could get Dad's watch while he was in the shower. Only this time I knew better than to go to Forty-second Street. It would be a lot safer to stay in my own neighborhood.

School seemed to last for an eternity. But finally the three o'clock bell sounded, and I headed home. Mom was busy in the kitchen. I sure didn't feel like talking, so I sat in front of the TV and watched the soaps.

Mom had supper on the table when Dad got home at six. Nobody said much at the table. I knew Dad was still seething inside.

I didn't eat much. When I asked to be excused and

started to leave the table, Dad let loose his blockbuster: "Jackie, your mother and I found her necklace today."

That was a lie! I knew where that necklace was—in a pawnshop in Manhattan. But I'd better play along. "Wonderful," I replied. "Where did you find it?"

Dad's hand came down on the table so hard that I jumped. "Listen," he yelled, "you know exactly where I found it—at a pawnshop in Manhattan. And I found the pawnshop ticket in your purse. Now tell me, why would you do something like that to your mother?"

I shifted my gaze to the floor, but I didn't answer.

"Don't just sit there!" Dad yelled. "I demand an answer from you! Why did you do that?"

When I ignored his demands and slowly stood up, he grabbed my arm and jerked me down into my chair again. Then I felt his hand across my face. "I said, answer me!" he screamed.

Feeling something on my cheek, I touched it and then looked at my hand. Blood!

I was furious. My mouth was swelling, and the pain was excruciating. Dad struck me across the face again. This blow was so hard it sent me reeling off the chair and onto the floor. I rolled over to shout something at him, but the words never got out of my mouth. He was down there on the floor, and this time his fist hit me square in the jaw.

I heard Mom screaming in the background, "Charles! Charles! Stop it! Stop it!"

Dad had jumped on top of me and was beating and yelling, "I'm not stopping anything until this little creep answers me. Now, Jackie, why did you do that to your mother and father?"

He had me pinned to the floor. I was no match for his strength. But I remembered how I had gotten old Randolph in the pawnshop last night. I let my spit fly, and it splattered right across his mouth!

It caught him totally by surprise, and he jumped up to wipe his mouth off. I rolled away from him, jumped up, and headed for the door. I called back to them. "Okay, I'll tell you why I did it. I'm a junkie! That's why!"

"You're a what?" Mom screamed.

"A junkie! A junkie! A junkie!"

"No! No! No!" she cried. "Tell me it isn't true."

I stepped over in front of her and raised my sleeve. "See that? See that hole in the middle of my arm? That's a fresh track. That ought to tell you something!"

Mom's mouth flew open, and she burst into tears.

Dad exploded. "So help me, we'll not have any junkie living in this house!"

"Well, you've got one whether you like it or not!" I screamed.

Dad started toward me again, his hand raised to hit me. When Mom tried to stop him, he let her have it instead.

I took off, and he tried to follow me. Mom grabbed him, screaming, "Charles! Charles! Can't you see what your daughter has gotten herself into? She's on drugs! We've got to do something to help her!"

"All junkies ought to be dead," he returned. "She's no good. She's probably out prostituting to support her habit. I won't have it in my house!"

"Keep your mouth shut, Charles! That girl needs help!"

I hurried to the bathroom and locked the door behind me. My face hurt terribly, and my lips were still dripping blood. I grabbed some toilet paper to wipe them off and caught a glimpse of myself in the mirror. That brought the tears.

They streamed down my cheeks in what seemed like an unending flow. I couldn't believe the horrible situation I now seemed to be trapped in. My homelife had become intolerable.

I sat on the edge of the bathtub to nurse my wounds. As I did, I looked over toward the medicine cabinet and remembered that Dad kept his razor blades in there. If I killed myself, would anyone really care? I thought my dad would be relieved! So I stumbled to my feet, opened the medicine-cabinet door, and through my tears, reached for a razor blade.

5

With one of Dad's single-edged razor blades clutched tightly in my right hand, I made a fist with my left hand until the vein stood out at my wrist. Anticipating the feeling of the blade and the subsequent pain sent shivers down my spine. But I gritted my teeth, squeezing the razor blade tighter than ever. This was it!

I fleetingly wondered about cutting slowly, but I knew I had to slash quickly before I lost my nerve. So I laid my arm down on the counter and raised the blade to slash.

A sharp knock on the door distracted me, and I whirled around. Good! I had remembered to lock the door. It would take them awhile to find one of those metal pieces to bypass the lock. I had time.

The knock became more persistent. It was probably my dad, coming to beat me up some more. I grabbed the nearby clothes hamper and jammed it under the doorknob, just in case he tried to force his way in.

I got all ready again. Then I heard Mom yell, "Jackie!"

When I didn't respond, she yelled again, "Jackie, open up! I want to talk to you!"

"I don't want to talk," I called back. "Not to you. Not to Dad. Not to anybody. I'm in no mood to talk!"

"Please, Jackie," she begged. "Please don't be so upset.

Come on, now. Unlock that door."

"I'll be out in a couple of minutes," I called.

A couple of minutes. That would give me time to end this miserable life of mine. I flushed the toilet, then I placed my wrist on the counter again and grabbed the razor blade.

Suddenly the door banged open, and with a thud the hamper tumbled to the floor, strewing clothes all over the place. Startled, I turned to face my mother.

At that instant she saw the razor blade and screamed, "Jackie! Jackie! What are you doing?"

"What does it look like?" I shot back. "I'm going to kill myself!"

She lunged for my hand and the blade, but I jumped back, screaming, "You lay one finger on me, and I'm going to slash your pretty face!"

She threw her hands over her face in horror. "You wouldn't do something like that to your own mother, would you?"

"Don't push me!" I snarled. "Whoever would have thought that my own father would abuse me? But he did! And now I'm going to get even with you two. You want peace and quiet around here? Well, I'll be a corpse in a few minutes. Then you won't have to worry about me anymore. Then you can have all the peace and quiet you want. And so will I!"

I've never seen Mom react to anything the way she did in that next moment. Before I could begin to counter her actions, she reached over, grabbed the hamper, and started toward me. I tried to duck, but where could I go? Our tiny bathroom didn't leave me any room for maneuvering. The hamper caught me right across the chest and threw me off balance. I felt Mom grabbing my right arm.

I flopped onto the floor, with the hamper on top of me, and Mom on top of the hamper. "Drop that razor blade, or I'll choke all the air out of you!" she threatened.

I cursed. That did no good. So I spit. Missed. I tried it again. Missed again. I couldn't get my breath, and I discovered that I wasn't nearly as anxious to die as I thought I was!

"Get off me!" I wheezed. "Get off me, or you'll kill me!"

"You may be dead, but not by any razor blade," Mom responded.

I tried to lift my arm toward her face, but the hamper and Mom had me effectively pinned to the floor. I felt as though my ribs would crack any minute.

I let the blade slip to the floor. Mom retrieved it immediately. Then she got off the hamper and pulled the hamper off me.

I lay there, trying to get my breath. She stood over me and said, "Jackie, this whole mess has gone far enough. I think it's time we had a talk."

"What do you mean, gone far enough?" I responded, rolling over so I could sit up. "If you ask me, we've already gone too far!"

She moved over and shut the door. Then she sat on the edge of the tub, pulled the toilet seat down, and motioned for me to sit there.

I didn't feel like talking. My old man didn't care about me. My old lady didn't care. Nobody cared. So I'd find a way to punish them—and punish them good.

But Mom wanted to talk, and I was in no position to argue with her.

"Now, Jackie," she started, "let's go back to the beginning—my pearl necklace."

I guess I hadn't realized how much those pearls meant to her.

"This morning after you left for school, your father and I discussed the necklace again," Mom said. "He had a sneaking suspicion you had taken it. You know, you've always had a hard time hiding anything from your father."

I nodded. No sense in disagreeing on that point. It seemed as though from the time I was a toddler he could see right through me.

"He went up to your bedroom to look around," Mom continued. "I tried to stop him, but he insisted. A little bit later he yelled for me to come. He showed me that pawnshop ticket."

That stupid ticket! Why hadn't I thrown it away?

"Jackie, I've never seen a pawnshop ticket in all my life. Even then, I told your father that the ticket could be for something else. I still couldn't believe you would do something like that to us."

"Yes," I interrupted, "and I never would have believed that Dad would beat me the way he just did!"

"Dad said there was only one way to find out," she went on, totally ignoring my comment. "He said he was going down to that pawnshop and see what kind of merchandise you had hocked. He said he'd miss a day of work, if he had to. Jackie, you don't know what you've put your mother and father through today."

If they only knew the other half of the story!

"When we went into the pawnshop, I felt like a creep—real clammy all over. And that owner—he was a creep, too. I don't see how you could do business with somebody like that. Well, we walked up to the counter, and Dad said, 'Can I get my merchandise back?'

"The owner looked at the ticket and mumbled, 'Sure. Why not?'

"Well, he reached under the counter and pulled out my pearls! I recognized them right away. Then Dad said, 'My daughter brought these in here, didn't she?'

"The man said, 'I don't know whether or not it was your daughter. A girl about five-foot-two, with blonde hair, brought these in. Is she your daughter?'

"When he said that, we both became furious. Then Dad blurted out, 'So help me, when I get my hands on that girl, I'm going to slap her good.'

"And Jackie, I'll never forget what that man said. He said he hoped Dad did that. He said that he couldn't trust anybody these days—especially not kids. I couldn't believe that children today are ripping off their parents, but that's what the man said is happening!"

She let that sink in.

"I still could hardly believe you had done this," she went on. "How could you steal from your parents? Haven't we tried to get you everything you needed? How could you do it? How could you?"

"I told you," I responded emotionlessly. "I needed the money to buy drugs."

"Jackie, why do you take drugs?"

Startled by that question, I looked at her blankly. I'd never asked myself that question before, so I really didn't have a satisfactory answer. "I just like getting high, that's all," I told her.

"Don't you know where you're headed?" she asked. "Last year I went to a council on drug abuse at your school. It was at one of the PTA meetings. I learned a few things that I never imagined would ever happen in our home. They said that girls like you start out smoking pot; then they may snort cocaine; then they try the needle."

I didn't tell her, but they were right on so far.

"You know what happens next, Jackie? These girls end up as prostitutes! They end up as gangsters! They'll do anything to support their habit! They said they would even steal from their parents. But I never would have believed this would happen in our own home. I've tried to—"

"Oh, come off the soapbox, Mom," I chided. "All I

did was hock your pearls to get a little loan. You got the necklace back, didn't you?"

"Yes, but it cost us sixty dollars. And that's not the real issue, Jackie. What I have to know is whether you are hooked. If so, how bad is it?"

"No, I'm not hooked. I just wanted to throw a scare into you and Dad, that's all. That needle mark was from a safety pin I pricked myself with. I'm not hooked at all."

"But, Jackie, you screamed out that you are a junkie. Are you or aren't you?"

I laughed. "No, Mom, I'm really not. I smoked pot once, but it didn't do anything for me, and I'll never do it again. I was just trying to find some way to strike back at Dad. But I'm no junkie. Everything is going to be okay. I promise."

I watched her features, wondering whether she was buying my story.

"Jackie, I want to believe you. I really do. But. . . ." Her voice trailed off, and she got up to leave.

When she opened the bathroom door, there stood Dad, looking chagrined that he had been caught eavesdropping. But he quickly recovered and took charge by yelling, "Nancy, we have a monster on our hands! I was listening to every word of that conversation! That girl is not to be trusted! We're going to have to lock up everything around here from now on. I know she is hooked. I know a track when I see one. My kid brother was hooked. Now our own little baby is using the needle!"

Mom's hand went up to her mouth as the horror of that revelation dawned on her. "Jackie, did you tell me the truth?" she asked.

"Mom, I told you the truth," I answered. "Dad's the filthy liar!"

Before the words were out of my mouth, I realized I'd said the wrong thing. Dad stormed into the bathroom, pushing Mom out of the way. Then, *whap!* He came down hard on my face. I was still weak from the fights I had just had with both of them. The force of the blow spun me around, and I went careening into the wall. My knees buckled, and I slumped to the floor, banging my head hard as I fell. I thought I was viewing a Fourth of July spectacular fireworks display. Then blackness.

When I opened my eyes, Dad was straddling me, his fists clenched. Mom was screaming, "Charles, if you hit her again, it will be the last thing you ever do!"

"She's a filthy, no-good junkie!" Dad yelled back at her, his curses turning the air blue. "She's probably been out shacking up with every bum in this town and is filled with disease! She's the scum of the earth!"

Oh, how I wanted to leap up off that floor, go for that razor blade, and slash that man's throat. Nobody was going to talk about me that way and get by with it. But I knew it was impossible. He was too big, too strong. And I wasn't about to take another rap on the head like that last one. My mouth smarted. My head ached. And I felt as though everything in my stomach was about to come up.

Dad backed off and headed for the living room. I heard the TV click on. Maybe he would watch something that would soothe his nerves long enough to get him off my case. At the moment, I wasn't concerned about violence on TV; I was concerned about it in my own home. My dad could play the lead in a monster movie!

Mom knelt beside me, gently put her arm underneath my aching head, and pulled me up close. She began to stroke my cheeks, sobbing as she did. "Jackie, I am so sorry for you, darling. I don't know what we're going to do."

We? What did she mean by that?

She leaned close to my ear. "Your father is getting totally unreasonable," she whispered. "Lately he's been slapping me around, too. I just don't know if I can take it much longer."

I looked up and saw the tears trickling down her cheeks.

"Oh, Mom," I cried, "I'm sorry. I had no idea. . . ."

I reached up and began to wipe away her tears as she went on: "He's becoming so mean and hateful, Jackie. If this keeps up, I'm going to have to move out. You can go with me. We're not about to put up with abuse like this."

Just then I heard Dad walking down the hallway. I knew I'd better get up, or he was likely to come in and kick me. I tried to steady myself against the sink as he came by and looked in the door.

"You'll be okay in a couple of days," he told me grandly. "You're just lucky I didn't split your head open!"

With that, he walked on by. He didn't seem to see—or to care—that Mom was crying. He *was* a monster.

I walked out into the hallway and up the stairs to my bedroom. I had to be alone to try to sort things out. What Mom had said put a new focus on things.

I eased onto my bed, hoping to stop the pounding in my head. Flat on my back, I stared at the ceiling, wondering what I was going to do now, wondering what was going to become of me.

I guess I must have dozed off, for when I looked at my watch, it was half-past twelve. My folks would be in bed by now. The house was quiet.

Did I have to face school in the morning? No way. Did I have to stay here and get slapped around? No way! But how could I get out of both of those situations? Mom had talked about leaving Dad. Hey—leaving. That was my answer! I'd leave home now!

I slipped off the bed and stumbled over to my closet, where I stored my small suitcase—the one I used when I spent a night at a girl friend's house. I packed a few things I figured I would need. I heard the mantle clock strike one, and I slowly opened my bedroom door. Shoes in hand, I tiptoed down the stairs. *Creak!* I stopped and listened. The only noise was Dad's rhythmic snoring.

I made it to our front door and eased it open ever so slowly. I stepped through and quietly shut it behind me. Then I tiptoed down the steps and onto the sidewalk, still carrying my shoes. Halfway down the block I turned and looked back at our house. It was completely dark. I had escaped!

Overjoyed and relieved, I leaned up against a wall and slid my shoes on, then hurriedly covered the remaining block and a half to the subway. I knew I had to be careful. At this hour all the muggers, junkies, and prostitutes were out.

As I started down the steps to the subway, it occurred to me that I had escaped—but where was I going? Why not Times Square? People were always around there.

After about forty-five minutes on the subway I got off at the Forty-second Street station, climbed up to the street, and started walking aimlessly. Where should I go? Maybe if I just stood around and watched the action, I'd get an idea.

I took a few more steps, and then I saw him—Michael Burke, leaning up against a wall.

Startled and scared, I quickly turned and started walking away as fast as I could. But when he realized who I was, he started running after me.

Dumb me! Why, of all the places on earth, did I have to come back here? I was sure Michael figured I had ripped off his bags of dope. He would never believe that I had been robbed. Every courier used that excuse!

My suitcase impeded my progress, so I let go of it and

took off running. I glanced around and realized he was gaining on me.

I put on a full head of steam, but it wasn't enough. I could almost feel his breath on my neck. His fingers tightened around my throat. He jerked, and we both tumbled to the pavement.

"Michael! Michael!" I screamed. "It wasn't my fault! It wasn't my fault!"

"Shut up!" he whispered. "Don't say another word!"

I looked over his shoulder and spotted a burly cop headed toward us. "Now what in the world is going on here?" he asked in a delightful Irish brogue. "Is this a boy-girl fight? Or is this a mugging?"

Michael jumped to his feet and brushed himself off. I struggled to get up, and he helped me.

"Officer," Michael said, "am I ever glad to see you! I'm Paul Yost, and this is my sister Patricia. You see, officer, I've been tailing her from Queens. She's run away from home, and I just found her. I had to knock her down to get her to stop. I'm taking her back home."

What was Michael doing? Was he trying to get rid of this cop so he could kill me?

But what was I going to do about it? If I said it was a lie, the cop would want to know what I was doing around here. And maybe he'd send me to a juvenile home—and then back to my parents! I'd better play along with Michael's story.

I turned on the tears. That was always one of my best acts. "Yes, officer, that's right," I sobbed. "I had this big fight with my parents, so I ran away. Right over there is my suitcase. If it's okay with you, I'll go get it and go home with Paul."

Michael was grinning. I had made it sound good. I hoped it would work.

"You're very lucky, young lady," the cop preached at me. "There are all kinds of pimps around here, ready to pounce on somebody like you. You sure look innocent. So you both get out of here quickly, before I have to run you in."

Michael gallantly took my arm and walked me toward my suitcase. He even picked it up and carried it as we walked down the block together. The officer, suspicious, followed us.

I leaned toward Michael and whispered, "Listen, I don't know what you are up to. But so help me, two thugs ripped off those drugs. They followed me all the way from your place. Michael, you've got to believe me."

"Sshh!" he cautioned. "Don't say anything else. If that cop hears what we're talking about, it's all over for both of us!"

"But Michael," I pleaded, "you've got to believe me!"

He tightened his grip on my elbow, digging his fingernails in. "Shut up!" he ordered. "And I mean, shut up!"

We quickened our pace and moved wordlessly toward the subway entrance at Forty-second Street. I glanced back and noticed the officer had gone another way. The moment of truth was upon me!

At the bottom of the stairs, Michael spun me around and backed me against the wall.

"Michael! Michael! Please believe me! Two brutes followed me from your place. I didn't wait where you said because I thought they had probably killed you."

"Were both of them over six feet tall, and did one of them have on a brown coat and the other a black coat?"

I tried to recall. I knew they were big. But when you're five-foot-two, anything looks huge. I was too scared to notice how they were dressed, but it did seem as though his description was accurate.

"Do you know them?" I asked.

"You'd better believe I know them. They're part of the Angeledo gang, and they're mean dudes. Those two turkeys have been threatening me. They claim I've been muscling in on their business. Well, as far as I'm concerned, the drug business is open to anybody. Anyway, I'll bet those two dudes called us last night. They were probably right outside and suspected you might carry drugs. What did they do to you?"

"Do to me?" I yelled. "They almost killed me, that's all!"

"What about the drugs?"

"Michael, those guys knew I had the drugs. They took me down to the Village and emptied out my bra and my boots. I mean, not only was it humiliating but I was also scared to death. I don't think they would have thought twice about killing me if it served their purposes."

"You're right about that," Michael answered. "And so help me, if I ever see those guys, I'm going to kill them. They won't get away with threatening me."

"Michael, do you know what you're saying?" I asked. "You just told me they were part of the mob. If you kill those guys, other brothers in the mob will get you. There's no way out. If I were you, I'd forget the whole thing."

"Yes, I guess you're right," Michael agreed. "No way am I going to tangle with the mob."

Just then, we heard someone descending the steps, and turned to see two policemen heading our way. Michael took off without a word. I didn't know why, but I ran, too. The cops, with their guns drawn, went right on by me, shouting, "Stop, or we'll shoot!"

I stopped, but they kept running after Michael. He vaulted the turnstile, jumped off the platform, and ran down into the darkness of the subway tunnel. That crazy idiot! Didn't he know the subway had a high-voltage rail? If he touched that rail, he'd be electrocuted! I held my breath.

The two cops were right behind him, yelling, "Stop, or

we'll shoot!" I waited, but I heard no shot. The three of them disappeared into the darkness.

I knew I'd better get out of there before those cops came back. If they picked me up, they'd want me to tell them where Michael's apartment was. So I ran up the exit stairs to Forty-second Street and headed toward Broadway. I glanced over my shoulder. No cops yet. Had Michael outrun them, too? Or was he now lying dead back there in that subway tunnel?

Out of breath, I leaned up against a building, shifting my suitcase to the other hand. I was so out of breath that I didn't notice a car stop at the curb near where I was resting. But I noticed when the guy rolled down the window nearest me and called, "Hey, baby, come here a minute."

I wondered what this well-dressed man was doing here and what he wanted. Had he lost his way after attending a play? His car glistened under the streetlights and flashing neon signs. It sure looked expensive.

Without pondering the consequences, I walked over to see what the guy wanted. That was one of the worst mistakes I ever made!

6

As I stepped toward the stranger's car, I noticed that it was a Rolls Royce! Wow! I had always drooled over fancy cars and dreamed that someday I would get to ride in something besides my dad's compact car.

I suspected that the guy might be a pimp, so I was going to have to be doubly careful.

He said something, but I didn't catch it, so I poked my head into the open window. I didn't want to get too far in, lest he activate the power window and trap me so he could kidnap me. I sure didn't want to be the slave of any pimp. So I just barely stuck my head in and asked, "What did you say?"

"Hey, little girl, going out on the town?"

I got my first good look at him. Wow! Was he ever handsome! I figured that pimps were mean and vicious, and didn't look anything at all like this. I guess that knocked my guard down a little.

"No, I just came into town," I said, laughing.

"Where are you from?"

Ohio was the first place that popped into my mind, so that's where I told him I was from.

"Ohio?" he echoed in surprise. "You've got to be kidding. That's where I'm from, originally."

A pimp from Ohio? That didn't fit, either. Pimps, I thought, came only from big cities.

Then he asked, "What city in Ohio?"

My mind went blank, and I kind of stammered and stuttered. The only city in Ohio I could remember hearing about was Cleveland, so I finally told him that's where I was from.

You should have heard him. He acted as though it were old home week. "I was born and raised in Cleveland!" he exclaimed excitedly. "Then I went to Ohio State University."

I was getting more and more uncomfortable and wondering how I was going to change the subject. But no way. He seemed determined to find out every last little detail because next he wanted to know, "What part of Cleveland?"

Here I was, considering myself fortunate that I was able to remember that Cleveland was a city in Ohio. I sure didn't know the names of the neighborhoods or housing developments. But I knew it stood to reason that every city would have a north, south, east, and west side, so I picked the south.

"Oh," he said, obviously disappointed. "I lived in the northeastern part, toward the lake. My parents had a very large home and quite a bit of property there."

I figured I'd better change the subject while I could, so I asked, "Where are you headed?"

"Well, I just got through a high-level business meeting," he answered. "You know, a dinner session that went on and on. But I've got to go down to Philadelphia. I just decided I'd go on down there tonight. I can save a little time by keeping out of the heavy traffic."

I looked him over carefully, as he was speaking. His suit seemed to be the latest designer fashion. I couldn't get over what an absolute doll he was. He somehow looked familiar. He was a real macho man. I decided that no way was this man a pimp. He sounded too honest—and looked too respectable. I thought he really was just a businessman going down to Philadelphia. I really didn't care where I went, as long as it was away from New York City.

"Philadelphia?" I asked excitedly. "Really? I was hoping to be able to get a ride down there. Do you mind if I ride along? I can talk to you and help you stay awake."

"Hey, that's a great idea," he responded. "The reason I stopped was that I noticed you had a suitcase, and I figured you were probably heading out of town. Almost everybody goes south, it seems. I just took a chance on you, and it looks as though it paid off. Come on, hop in. Let's get going!"

I couldn't believe it. First thing, I ran into a rich businessman! Maybe if I worked things right I could give him a sob story and get some money. I sure was going to need money if I was going to be out on my own.

I opened the car door, pushed my suitcase in, and waited while he tossed it into the backseat. Then I jumped in. The seat was so plush I felt as though I sank two feet in it!

We glided away from the curb. I was busy looking at all the gadgets and meters and the luxury decor. I could hardly believe it! Here I was, really riding in a Rolls Royce!

As we headed down Forty-second Street, the man smiled and asked, "What's your name?"

I almost gave him a false one, but he seemed harmless enough, so I said, "Jackie Marshall."

Then I asked the obvious: "What's yours?"

"You don't recognize me?"

I shook my head.

"I'm Burt Reynolds."

Don't tell me! Not only was I riding in a Rolls but was

this a movie star as well? Was he the real Burt Reynolds? Maybe that's why he had seemed familiar when I first talked to him.

"Are you the real Burt Reynolds, the movie star?"

"In the flesh."

If I hadn't been sitting in a car, I'd have jumped a mile high, I was so excited. Here I was, alone with a famous movie sex symbol! Oh, how I wanted to reach over and grab him. If he would kiss me, my world would be complete! Then I could go back to my school and tell all the girls that I had had a date with Burt Reynolds! Wow! This had to be a dream!

I slid over toward him, trying not to be too obvious. I knew Burt Reynolds had the reputation of being a great lover. If he would just give me one passionate kiss, I'd be satisfied. I mean, nobody would ever believe me, but I'd know!

We had gone only a few blocks when two policemen stopped us and motioned us to the curb.

"What's this all about?" I asked.

"I don't know," he responded. "They're probably checking registrations. I've been stopped before, especially when I'm out late like this. Sometimes they just assume that a Rolls has to be stolen. And Rolls owners don't really mind their keeping close tabs on the cars."

As one cop walked toward us, I couldn't help but smile to myself because I was thinking about how surprised he was going to be when he looked at the driver's license and saw that he had stopped Burt Reynolds! And I was with him! I felt so important.

Burt pushed the button to lower the window. "May I see your driver's license and registration, please?" the cop asked.

Burt fumbled through some papers in the glove compartment and handed the cop the registration.

"And your driver's license, please," the cop repeated.

Burt pulled his wallet out of his hip pocket. It was fat with money. That figured.

I was so excited about the scene I knew was about to transpire that it almost bowled me over when the cop said, "Mr. Simpson, do you mind telling me what you're doing in the area this time of night?"

Had that cop said "Mr. Simpson"? Couldn't he read?

"I just came from a dinner meeting with a few of my movie associates," Burt said. "I'm heading toward Philadelphia. Why? Is something wrong, officer?"

"No, not really. But who is the young lady with you?"

I held my breath. Would Burt tell him I was a runaway?

"This is my younger sister Kathy," Burt told the officer. "We're going down to visit my mother in Philadelphia. She's been very ill—so ill that Kathy and I figured we'd better go down tonight. We don't know how much longer she's got."

Not only was Burt a great actor but he was also a great liar!

The cop handed the papers back and apologized, "Excuse the interruption, Mr. Simpson. Hope your mother is all right."

Why did that officer keep calling Burt "Mr. Simpson"? Was that his real name and Burt Reynolds his stage name?

As he started driving again, I asked, "How come that cop called you Mr. Simpson? Do you have an alias?"

Burt began to laugh. "Jackie, I'm not really Burt Reynolds. I've been told I look like him, but my name really is Don Simpson."

"Don Simpson?"

"Yes. But Burt Reynolds has nothing on me," he said, recognizing my disappointment. "I'm a better lover than he is!"

I didn't like the way he said *lover*. Maybe after we got

to Philadelphia, he'd try something. I scooted back toward my window.

When we got to the Westside Highway, he turned north. Oh, oh! Philadelphia was south! "How come we're not going through the Lincoln Tunnel and heading south?" I asked.

"You know New York City pretty well," he said, "almost like a native."

I gulped. After all, I told him I had just gotten in from Ohio. "Oh, I have a good sense of direction," I stammered.

"Well, if it will put your sweet little mind at ease," he said, "I've got to stop by my apartment. This morning I bought my mother a little gift, and I forgot to bring it along when I went to this meeting. If I don't give it to her tonight, I may never get a chance to give it to her. You don't mind if I stop there for a minute, do you?"

What could I say? If I objected, all he would have to do would be to tell me to get out. And how could I object to someone who wanted to do something for his dying mother? Besides, this whole thing was just too exciting. Even if he weren't Burt Reynolds, this still was a real Rolls Royce, and I was thoroughly enjoying riding in it. And I figured if he tried anything, I could handle him.

As we rode along, I felt so important and so rich. I wondered how rich people sat in a car like this, and I straightened up and tried to look rich.

But as usually happens when you're trying to impress someone, in my scooting I knocked my purse onto the floor, and the contents scattered. Mr. Simpson had to brake suddenly at that point, and some of the stuff rolled forward, and then back underneath the seat.

When I reached underneath the seat to retrieve my makeup, my hand touched something cold and hard. At first I thought it was part of the seat mechanism. But then I touched it again. It was unmistakably a gun!

I jerked back up in the seat and looked at Don questioningly. "What's the matter?" he asked.

What was he doing with a gun? If he had lied to me about his identity, would he also lie about the gun? Was this guy some kind of a crook? Who was he, anyway?

I decided I'd better not mention the gun, so I said, "I didn't know they put plush carpeting so far back under the seat in these cars."

He laughed easily. "For the price I had to pay for this, they should have carpeted the outside, too!"

Relieved that I had gotten out of that one, I laughed along with him. Then I remembered his mission and I asked, "Is your mom really pretty bad off?"

"Yes, she's about gone. She's had cancer for years now. In fact, this morning when I called, the doctor said it had spread all through her body. That's why I want to get down there tonight. The doctor said that at any moment she could slip off into a coma. He said he didn't think she'd last through the week."

The words were all right, but the situation was all wrong. Somebody whose mother was about to die ought to be more distraught, I decided. He was handling it almost casually.

But I decided it would be wise for me to be sympathetic. "I'm sorry to hear that, Don," I said. "Isn't there anything else the doctors can do?"

He nodded sadly. "There comes a time, Jackie," he said sadly—and with more feeling now—"that all the money in the world won't buy a person another minute of life. I'm afraid Mom is about to reach that point. We've done everything we can for her. Frankly, I'll be a little relieved when she goes—at least then she won't be suffering so."

I guessed I had read him wrong, so I just sat quietly. He didn't seem to want to talk about it anymore.

We exited at Seventy-second Street, drove over to Broadway, and stopped in front of an exquisite apartment house. The building sure fit with the Rolls!

"It's going to be a long evening yet," Don said. "Why don't you come up to my apartment for just a minute? You could freshen up. Besides, I love to show off my apartment."

What did I have to lose? And I sure wanted to see the kind of apartment a rich man like Don lived in.

The doorman met us as we got out of the car. Don introduced me again as his younger sister Kathy. That really didn't bother me. I figured it was none of the doorman's business.

I was admiring the beautiful lobby when I happened to glance out the door and notice the Rolls driving away.

"Don," I yelled, "someone just drove away in your Rolls!"

He laughed. "That's just Alex, the doorman. He's taking it to the parking lot."

"Parking lot? I thought we were just going to be here for a minute."

He smiled, but didn't answer. He just pushed the button for the elevator. But I was getting mighty nervous. When the elevator door opened and he motioned me inside, I headed for the front door. Don grabbed my elbow and asked, "What's the matter?"

"Mr. Simpson," I said, "I think I'd better be on my way. I don't think I'd better drive to Philadelphia with you."

"Hey, Jackie, come on. There's no problem. This will just take a minute. Then we'll be on our way."

I stood my ground, so he asked, "What are you afraid of? Don't you believe I'm for real?"

"No, I don't," I blurted out, forgetting what little I knew about tact. "What I've seen has already scared me to death, and I've decided to get out while I still can."

He reached for his wallet. "Here, let me show you some identification." He stuck his driver's license up for me to see. "Look there—I'm Donald Simpson. And it's this address."

Yes, it was just as he said. But that didn't solve all my problems. I might as well have it out with him, I decided.

"Okay, Mr. Simpson, first you told me you were Burt Reynolds, but I found out you're Donald Simpson. Second, that cop stopped us, and that scared me. Then when I happened to reach under the seat in your car, I felt a gun. You said we were going to Philadelphia. Instead we came here, to your apartment. You said we would just be here a minute, but no sooner did we get inside than your car was driven away. Something about this whole thing is fishy."

The light on the elevator was flashing because the door had stayed open so long, so Don took his hand away. Then he turned to me and smiled— the kind of smile that could melt stone!

"Jackie, Jackie," he said. "I can see that some things might look suspicious to someone as sharp as you are—someone who's got it all together. But there's a good explanation for each one of those things."

He led me over to some chairs, and we sat as he set about to relieve my fears.

"First, let's talk about that cop," he said. "I've got a pretty good idea why he stopped us. I know you just got into town, so you wouldn't be aware of this. But in a city like New York, there's a lot of pimps around. You know what a pimp is, don't you?"

I nodded.

"Well, these pimps often drive big, expensive cars. I think that cop was checking me out. After all, we were down in an area where a lot of prostitutes operate, and most law-abiding citizens are in bed at this hour. It was a logical check. And I know that when a cop stops you, there's no sense arguing. The same kind of thing has happened to me three times before.

"Now as far as going to Philadelphia: My mother really is sick. If you want, when we get up to my apartment, I'll call her and you can talk to her. In fact, maybe you could cheer her up a little."

He paused, watching my reaction.

"Now as far as that gun is concerned, you have to understand something about being rich. There's a price to pay. Suppose, Jackie, you were going to rob somebody. You're not going to try to hold up some bum on the Bowery. You're going to go for somebody who looks rich—like a guy driving a Rolls Royce. Well, I know that, too. That's why I have to carry a gun—for my own protection.

"Let's see," he said. "Seems there was something else. Oh, yes. The doorman's driving off with the car when I said we were only going to be here for a few minutes. I'm sure that did seem strange to you. But here again, you have to understand the problems of being rich. If I left that Rolls on the street, it wouldn't last for five minutes. Professional car thieves can break into almost any car, start the engine, and drive off in less than a minute! So Alex and I have this understanding—I give him a nice tip once a month for this—that whenever I drive up, whether I plan to be in the apartment for two minutes or two days, he always puts the car in the parking garage. That's why you saw him drive off. Satisfied?"

I felt so embarrassed. Every one of his explanations was totally logical. I must be overreacting. What could I say?

Don took me by the arm and led me back to the elevator. We got off at the fifth floor, walked down the hallway, and he opened a door. I stepped into luxury I never even imagined existed! I couldn't get over the gorgeous drapes, plush carpeting, expensive, overstuffed furniture, and bold, modern art. I'd seen pictures of places like this, but here I was, standing in one. Everything here spelled M-O-N-E-Y!

I walked over to the window and looked out at the sparkling lights of New York City. Then a woman's voice startled me as I heard, "Don, who's the chick?"

I spun around to see a tall, shapely girl talking to Don. Who was she? Where had she come from? And what was she doing here?

"Jackie, this is my wife, Juanita," Don said, noticing my puzzled look. "Juanita, this is Jackie Marshall."

His wife? Why hadn't he mentioned her? She looked like one of those tall, willowy models that you see in fashion magazines—the kind and shape that it seems they make all the clothes to fit. I stood there admiring her and secretly wishing I could be a little taller and look like that.

Then it hit me. Surely she wouldn't sit still for my riding to Philadelphia with her husband! I was no slouch as far as looks were concerned, and she would surely be aware of that!

While all these thoughts were going through my mind, Juanita was walking over and extending her hand. As she moved, I became aware of her flowing nightgown that made her look like something out of a dream.

"Glad to have you here," Juanita said. "Hope you enjoy your stay."

My stay? Now why would she say something like that? I had no intention of staying. She didn't seem surprised that Don had brought me up here. Did he do this kind of thing often? What kind of a strange marriage did these two have, anyway? I just couldn't sort it all out.

Suddenly another tall, beautiful girl appeared from down a hallway. "Anybody care for a drink?" she asked.

I looked at her, then at Juanita, then at Don. Quickly

he responded to my puzzled look by telling me, "Jackie, this is Juanita's sister Corrine. She's visiting us."

Then to Corrine he said, "This is Jackie Marshall. I found her down on Forty-second Street carrying a suitcase. She looked kind of lonely, so I offered her a ride."

Corrine smiled and stuck out her hand. She seemed so friendly.

"You're sure lucky that Don picked you up," she said. "I mean, there are some real mean dudes down in that area, you know. They're looking for cute little girls like you, Jackie."

Maybe I was lucky. After all, it sure was better to be in this rich businessman's apartment than out sleeping on the streets of New York City! And he wouldn't try anything funny with his wife and her sister there. But I still couldn't help but wonder why he hadn't told me about them. Was something wrong with this setup?

"Jackie, go ahead and sit down," Don said. "I'll be right with you. And you girls make her feel right at home, okay?"

He took off down the hall, and I plopped into one of those plush chairs. Juanita sat across from me, smiling, but apparently a little ill at ease over my presence. Corrine headed for the kitchen.

I guess I could understand what Juanita must be feeling—maybe a twinge of jealousy over Don's picking me up. Maybe she was wondering whether we had done anything wrong. Well, it was an awkward situation, to say the least. So I decided I'd better try to do something to ease it.

"Have you lived here long?" I asked.

"No, not really. A couple of years or so. Nice place, huh?"

"Fantastic!" I responded. "I've never been around such luxury in all my life. You're lucky to live here, Juanita."

She turned and stared out the window. I could sense she was deeply troubled over something. Maybe her marriage wasn't going so well, and my coming home with Don probably hadn't helped anything.

"What would you like to drink, Jackie?" Corrine yelled from the kitchen.

"Do you have a soda?"

"Yes. We have everything. You name it, we have it."

"You know the city?" Juanita asked.

"You mean New York City?"

"Yes. I mean, you've been out in the street for a while, haven't you? Have you been working for anybody?"

"You mean, do I have a job?"

Juanita laughed. "Well, I guess you might call it that. I mean, were you out on the street working for a pimp? You know, working on the streets?"

That made it plain enough. Juanita must have thought I was a prostitute! Maybe that's why she was upset about my coming up here with Don. After all, he had told her he picked me up on Forty-second Street, and a lot of prostitutes worked around there.

This time when I looked at her, she was staring right back at me. Somehow she didn't seem very friendly, now. And her questions were downright offensive to me.

"I don't know what you think I am," I replied angrily, "but if you think I'm a prostitute, you've got another thing coming!"

I said it more sharply than I had intended to say it, but I really didn't care. Nobody was going to infer I was a prostitute and get by with it.

But she just laughed. "My, you're a spunky little one, aren't you? But I wouldn't get my nose out of joint about prostitutes. Everybody's got to make a living. I don't see anything wrong with offering somebody a good time. Certainly I can't see anything wrong with prostitution if it's done tastefully."

Nothing wrong with prostitution? The very word was disgusting to me! Never would I get involved in something like that. And I thought a rich lady would have had better sense than to talk the way Juanita was talking. If this was sophistication, I wasn't sure I wanted any part of it.

Before I could respond, Corrine came in carrying my soda. About the same time, Don walked in and announced, "Jackie, I'm afraid I have some bad news. I just called my family in Philadelphia. My mother passed away."

"Oh, no! I am so sorry to hear that, Don. I really am."

"Well, that means I won't be going to Philadelphia tonight," Don went on. "But I would never hear of your going out on the street at this hour of the night. So I insist that you spend the night here with us. Then in the morning we can be on our way."

That sounded like a good deal. I sure didn't have anywhere else to go, and I was getting awfully tired from all I had been through.

"If it's not too much bother," I said, "it sure would be nice of you."

"Bother?" Don echoed. "Why, it would be our pleasure! I'll phone Alex and have him get your suitcase and bring it up. And, if you don't mind, I think I'll retire for the night. I know I'll have a busy day tomorrow with a lot of decisions to be made."

Just as Don walked back down the hallway, the phone rang. I listened as Corrine answered it. I thought maybe Don's family was calling with more information, and that would affect the time we left for Philadelphia tomorrow.

Corrine wrote something on the pad next to the telephone. I heard her repeat the address: "Hilton Hotel, room 1236."

When she hung up, she smiled broadly and said, "I have to go to work."

Work? At this hour? And at the Hilton? I was dying to ask what kind of work she did, but by the time I got up enough nerve, she was already out the apartment door.

Juanita didn't offer any explanation. She simply said, "Come on, Jackie. I know you must be exhausted. I'll show you your room. You're really going to like this!"

She led me down another hallway, and at the end she opened a door. I couldn't believe my eyes. There before me was a king-size canopied bed already turned down to reveal satin sheets. I spotted an armoire and a huge mirror and a large dresser.

"There's your own private bathroom, too," Juanita said expansively. "You'll enjoy this room. I think it's absolutely gorgeous."

Gorgeous? That was indeed an understatement. These people had to be rolling in wealth!

Just then, the apartment doorbell rang, and Juanita said, "It's probably Alex with your suitcase. Let me go see."

When she brought it in, my battered suitcase looked so out of place in the middle of this luxury.

But I still wondered about Corrine, and I finally got up enough nerve to ask Juanita.

Once again she got that funny look in her eyes. "Jackie," she said, "whatever we have here, we're willing to share with you. But there's one thing you've got to remember: Don't ask questions."

She turned on her heel, shut the door after her, and was gone.

But the way she had answered my question unsettled me even more. This whole setup seemed too good to be true. Yet I had this uneasy feeling that something was terribly wrong. What had I gotten myself into now?

7

I slipped into the gown I had brought in my suitcase and glanced at the digital clock on the nightstand. 4:12 A.M. It had been a long night, and I was really ready for sleep.

The soda had left me thirsty, so I headed into the bathroom for a glass of water. But there was no glass. I'd have to go to the kitchen.

I hadn't brought a bathrobe with me. Should I take my chances and dart to the kitchen? After all, only Juanita was around. I didn't expect to run into Don. He'd already gone to bed.

When I walked out in the hall, I noticed a light still burning in the living room. Hadn't Juanita gone to bed? Or had she just forgotten to turn out the light?

I tiptoed down the hall. When I was opposite the living room, I gasped. There was a man sitting in a chair, and he was staring at me.

"Hello," he said nonchalantly.

I hugged my arms up around me, wondering whether I should turn and run back to the bedroom. But I was also wondering what this guy was doing in Don's living room. He didn't look like a burglar.

"Where are you going?" he demanded.

I didn't like the way he asked that question—sharp and to the point. What business was it of his?

"Oh, I just wanted to get a drink of water, that's all."

"Okay, get it quickly and go back to bed."

For crying out loud! He sounded just like my father! Didn't he know I was a guest in this house?

"Hey, who do you think you are, anyway?" I responded testily.

He stood up, stretched, and walked toward me. He placed his fingers under my chin and pushed my face up toward his. He was so big and tall, and looked so mean. "I'm your guardian angel," he replied sarcastically.

I slapped his hand away. "Listen, buster, I don't know who you are, but you'd sure better tell me. Otherwise I'm going to start screaming that you tried to do something to me, and Mr. Simpson will come running with his gun."

Laughing, the big guy told me, "Mr. Simpson is gone."

"Gone?" I asked. "He was here when I went to bed."

"He got a call a few minutes ago. Said he'd be gone until about noon. Some kind of business deal."

"What about Corrine and Juanita?"

"They're both out taking care of some business, too."

"Do you mean these people are all out taking care of business at this hour of the night?"

He laughed again—that same sarcastic kind of laugh that tied knots in my stomach. "What's the matter, little girl? Are you a detective or something? Don't ask so many questions!"

I sure didn't feel thirsty now. I thought I'd better head back to my bedroom before this punk got ideas. I sure didn't like the feeling of being here alone with him!

Better yet, why didn't I head back to my bedroom and get dressed and get out of this place? I couldn't put my finger on it yet, but I knew that something just wasn't right about this whole situation.

Without another word, I retreated to the bedroom,

quickly got dressed, grabbed my suitcase, and stepped out into the hall. But this time the big guy was standing there waiting, almost as though he had been reading my mind.

"Where are you going?" he demanded.

"None of your business!" I retorted.

"You aren't going anyplace!"

"Who's going to stop me? You get out of my way before I scream!"

He laughed—that same sarcastic, sinister laugh. "Mr. Simpson hired me to guard his apartment," he said. "He told me nobody was to come in, and nobody was to go out. So, little girl, I don't want to make it rough on you, but there's no way you're going to leave this place. I have my orders."

"What are you talking about?" I roared. "I'm a guest here. I'm no prisoner. I can come and go as I—"

"Of course you're a guest," he interrupted. "Of course you're not a prisoner. All I know is that I have my orders. You can't leave now. You'll have to wait until the others get back."

"Who are you, anyway?" I asked, puzzled over this strange turn of events.

"Mr. Simpson hired me to guard his apartment. There have been some break-ins and that kind of stuff around here, so I guess you might just call me an armed guard." He stressed that word *armed*. "And Mr. Simpson told me to look out for you. So I'm doing exactly what he said. And that means there is no way you can leave at this hour of the night."

What was I going to do? Obviously I couldn't arm wrestle this thug into submission. So I really didn't have much choice. I'd just go back to bed and take my chances tomorrow with Don or Juanita.

"Okay, mister, have it your way," I said as I walked back to my bedroom.

Once again I took off my jeans and put on my gown. I slipped between those satin sheets, and the luxury of the situation quickly overcame my anxieties. Before I knew it, I was fast asleep.

When I awakened the next day, it was with quite a start! Someone was stirring around in my room!

I sat up, pulling the sheets around me, because there stood Don Simpson.

"Well, good morning, Jackie," he said brightly. "How was your night?"

"Well, I slept just fine," I said, "but I had a horrible experience before I went to bed."

"Horrible? What happened?"

"Some big guy threatened me and wouldn't let me leave."

"Oh, you must be talking about Gregory, my night guard. I told him you were here. He didn't try anything funny, did he?"

"Well, no. But I decided I'd better get out of here, and he wouldn't let me go."

"Of course he wouldn't let you leave, Jackie," Don purred. "Why, I would never have forgiven him if he had. Don't you know that it's like a jungle out there? This isn't Ohio!"

Before I could respond that I could take care of myself, a cute little poodle puppy came bouncing into the bedroom, jumped right up into bed with me, and began licking my face. Immediately it had my heart!

I grabbed it and hugged it close. "What a darling puppy," I said. "Whose is it?"

Don smiled. "It's yours."

"Mine?"

"That's what I said. It's all yours. I was out this morning, and just happened to go by a pet shop. Well, I saw this little poodle that looked like it needed a friend. I think it's already decided to adopt you!"

I couldn't believe anybody would do something so nice for me! I had never been able to have any kind of a pet before.

"What's his name?" I asked, after I had thanked him profusely for his kindness.

"Well, first of all, he's a she," Don laughed. "And she doesn't have a name yet. What would you like to call her?"

I held the puppy up at arm's length as I studied her features. She was wiggling and trying to get at my face again. It was then I was aware, for the first time, of the bright red bow around her neck. That gave me an idea. "I'm going to call her Ribbons."

"Hey, Jackie, that's a cute name. A cute name for a cute little dog for a cute little girl. Now why don't you hurry and get dressed and bring Ribbons into the kitchen with you for some breakfast. You're both probably starved."

Don shut the door after him. I quickly showered while Ribbons had a great time carrying one of my sneakers around. She was so cute, so playful—and all mine! I couldn't believe it!

I quickly dressed and walked down the hall. Ribbons must have decided my sneakers were her own special playthings because she kept tugging on them, even though I was wearing them.

When I walked into the kitchen, I was startled to meet still another woman.

"Hi, I'm Jackie Marshall," I said pleasantly. "Who are you?"

"Oh, I'm just a friend of Don."

This was really a strange place!

Because she was busy fixing breakfast, I wondered if she was the maid. When I asked her that, she replied, "Well, I guess you could say I work for Don Simpson."

"What's your name?" I asked.

"Yolanda."

She didn't volunteer any additional information. Under other circumstances I probably would have asked. But Ribbons was bouncing up and down all over the kitchen.

"Do you want some breakfast?" Yolanda asked.

"I sure would. I'm starved."

"Coming right up. And Don bought some puppy food, so I guess your little dog can have something to eat, too."

I helped Yolanda fix Ribbons' food and then ate the delicious breakfast this strange woman had fixed for me. She didn't eat. She just sat there drinking coffee and looking blankly around.

I didn't know what to talk about, but she seemed interested in Ribbons, so I said, "After breakfast, I think I'll take Ribbons for a walk outside."

Yolanda's mouth dropped open. "Oh, no, Jackie! You can't do that!"

"What do you mean?" I responded. "What's wrong with taking a puppy for a walk? It's the middle of the day. There certainly aren't any muggers on the street now."

"You'll have to talk to Mr. Simpson first."

What was going on here, anyway? Last night that man wouldn't let me leave. Now I just wanted to take my dog for a walk, and Yolanda was acting as though I'd asked permission to go rob a bank! Permission—that was it. I wished these people would quit treating me like a little kid. I was on my own now. I could make my own decisions.

"Yolanda, let's get something straight," I said curtly. "Maybe you work for Don Simpson, but I don't. I'm just here as his guest. And it's making me nervous that nobody wants me to leave!"

Yolanda gasped. "Don't try anything, Jackie, or you

might be sorry. I mean, real sorry."

Before I could ask what she meant by that, Don walked into the kitchen. "Have a good breakfast?" he asked.

I nodded, complimenting Yolanda's cooking. Then I said, "Mr. Simpson, I can't figure this place out. You were kind to me and gave me this cute little puppy. I told Yolanda I was going to take Ribbons for a walk, and she said I had to ask you for permission before I went outside. I think it's time we got something straight. You're not my old man. I went through enough of that kind of thing. That's why I'm not at home now. I'm a big girl. I'm old enough to make my own decisions. I can come and go as I please."

"Jackie, Jackie. Calm down, will you?" Don soothed. "Of course you can come and go as you please. Why, if you want to, you can walk out that door right now. You can even take Ribbons with you. I guess you said you were heading to Philadelphia. Well, you can head out right now, if that's the way you want it. Right, Yolanda?"

Yolanda shifted uneasily in her chair and avoided my gaze as she answered, "Sure, Mr. Simpson. She can leave right now."

I breathed a sigh of relief. "Oh, thank you, Don," I said. "You've been very kind to me, and I appreciate all you've done for me, but I can't impose on you any longer."

I grabbed Ribbons, who immediately started licking my face. At least I had a cute little dog—probably an expensive one, too.

"Go ahead back to your bedroom," Don suggested. "But I hope you won't leave until I've had a chance to talk to you. I'll be there in a minute."

Back in the bedroom, I packed my suitcase and sat on the edge of the bed to wait. I waited and waited for the better part of an hour Now I was really getting nervous. Why didn't he come? I hated to leave when he had asked me to wait. After all, he had been very kind to me. But there was a limit to—

Just then, he knocked on the door and walked in, carrying beautiful jeans, blouses, sneakers, and shoes—a whole, absolutely gorgeous wardrobe. I quickly noticed that everything seemed to be in my size.

"These are for you, Jackie," he said. His eyes brimmed with pleasure, like a parent watching a child open a Christmas package.

I stared unbelievingly. "All these are for me? How come?"

"Well, Jackie, you have won our hearts," he said. "And I wanted to get you to stay long enough so I could tell you the truth about this place. Can I do that now?"

"Could you tell me the truth? Oh, I wish you would! I'm just dying of curiosity!"

"I don't quite know how to say this," he started, "but you might as well know that Juanita and I can't have any children of our own. And I've always wanted a child. Well, last night when I picked you up, I fell in love with you. Not a man-woman kind of love, but a father-daughter kind of love, you know? I mean, you're the kind of daughter that Juanita and I have always dreamed of having. I couldn't believe I had you in the car with me and that you came up here to our apartment. Well, last night Mrs. Simpson and I talked it over. We were wondering, Jackie, if you wouldn't just live here with us, and be like a daughter to us. As you probably guessed, I've got lots of money, so I can buy you a lot more nice things like those clothes. You can go with us to fancy restaurants, Broadway plays, and travel to exotic places. We'll take good care of you."

Don watched as I fondled the clothes: designer jeans, silk blouses, expensive shoes. It was obvious that Don had a lot of money. So he wanted to spend a little of it on me—why not? Why shouldn't I be like his daughter? I had to be the world's biggest jerk for thinking about running out on a one-in-a-million situation like this!

"Well, Mr. Simpson, if you really do feel that way, I think I'm going to take you up on your offer."

He came over and hugged me. "Welcome home, daughter," he said softly. "I've waited a long time for you."

Ribbons was tearing around, jumping up and down. Maybe she understood that she had found a wonderful new home!

The next couple of days passed by rather routinely. Don didn't say anything about going to Philadelphia, and that made me wonder. And there were other girls coming and going. I learned that they were models. That's why he had all these attractive girls around. I also learned that this was just one of his many businesses.

The Simpsons made me feel right at home. I had anything I wanted. But whenever I went anywhere, I always had to have one of the other girls with me. They said it was for my protection, and I believed them. But this protectiveness was beginning to smother me. I didn't like being treated like a little girl again.

After two weeks I was really getting used to living like the rich, and I decided to live with the Simpsons forever. Don lived up to all his promises. Night after night we went to expensive restaurants and Broadway plays.

About a month later, when I went into the kitchen one morning to fix my breakfast, Corrine walked in. Her face looked horrible! "What happened?" I asked.

She didn't respond, just walked on by and poured herself a cup of coffee.

Don walked in and I asked, "Have you seen Corrine? She looks as though she needs to see a doctor."

He ignored me and ordered Corrine back to her room.

She took her coffee and walked out without a word.

"Mr. Simpson, who in the world beat her up?" I asked.

"I did," he replied matter-of-factly.

I jumped up from my hardly touched breakfast. "You beat up Corrine? Why?"

"She tried to keep back some of the money."

What did he mean by that?

"Jackie," he went on, "I think it's time for us to have a father-daughter talk. Let's go to your bedroom."

He didn't say anything as we walked to my room. I sat on the edge of the bed, waiting. He stood in front of me.

"I really thought you would have caught on by this time," he started. "I operate a house of prostitution."

I jumped off the bed. "A house of prostitution? This doesn't look like a house of prostitution!"

"I don't mean this apartment," he replied. "I mean, I have a number of girls working for me. And I expect you to work for me, too."

"Mr. Simpson, for crying out loud, I'm no prostitute!" I said in disbelief.

He smiled. "Of course you're not. None of my girls is a prostitute. They're just girls who perform a service and get well paid for it. I put them up in good apartments. I give them everything they need. And all of us do very well."

The word *prostitution* nauseated me. "Absolutely no way!" I told him. "I'm just not that type of girl."

"Don't tell me you're not that type of girl," he sneered. "I noticed your needle marks. You've used drugs. And Jackie, drugs will kill you. If you stay with prostitution, you'll live happily ever after."

I hadn't had any drugs since I came here. There was no way I could get them.

"I have used drugs in the past," I admitted. "But I will never get involved in prostitution. No way!"

"You *are* involved!" he snarled, and slapped my face hard.

I tried to spin away, but he grabbed my arm firmly. "You'll start tonight, Jackie, whether you like it or not!"

What was happening to me? I was trapped. Now when I looked at Don Simpson, I realized I was looking into the eyes of a pimp! Everything he had told me was lies! Lies! How could I be so naive and get myself into a mess like this?

"I can't do it!" I protested.

"Oh, yes, you can!" he replied. "Do you remember what Corrine looked like? I did that to her because she tried to hold back some of her earnings. And that's what is going to happen to you if you give me the least bit of trouble. There's no more of this phony daughter bit. From now on you are working for me, just like Corrine and Juanita and—"

"Juanita? She works for you? I thought she was your wife!"

He laughed. "She's just like all the others."

"And suppose I decide not to take you up on your offer of employment," I said sarcastically.

I shouldn't have said that. *Slap!* His hand caught the side of my face sharply. "That's the first!" he declared. "You have no choice. You're working for me!"

He yelled for Corrine to come. "She'll take you out this evening," he said, "and show you how it's done. I guess in the meantime she'd better tell you the things to watch for."

Corrine was right there. I wanted to scream that no way would I ever do anything like this. But one look at Corrine told me I really didn't have any choice.

When Corrine and I were alone, I asked, "Am I dreaming, or is this really happening to me?"

"You'd better believe it's happening," she replied. "Don Simpson is one of the meanest pimps in town. But the guy's a great actor. He can put up a front and snare all kinds of people. We're all caught in his trap."

"That's what you think!" I retorted. "There's no way I'm going to get into bed with some stranger. There's no way any guy is going to catch me!"

"Jackie, Jackie. I feel so sorry for you," she sympathized. "When I saw you walk in here that first night, I almost went out of my mind. You're so young. You have so much potential. And here you are, trapped in the snare of prostitution."

"Corrine, I just can't believe it. You know how well I have been treated here. Don's done everything for me. He's treated me like his own daughter. I can't believe he'd beat you up. I can't believe he'd hit me."

"Well, it's true, Jackie. We were all wondering how long it would be before he told you the awful truth. You had a lot longer reprieve than anyone else has ever had."

"How did he trap you?" I asked.

"Well, I used to work for a big ornery pimp named Phil Deacon. He was mean. If I didn't make enough, he'd split my lip. One night I took some of the money I'd earned and bought drugs. I mean, I got higher than a kite. Old Deacon beat me until I was almost dead. Then he sold me—just like a slave. He got one thousand bucks for me. Can you imagine? That's all I'm worth: one thousand dollars! He sold me to Don Simpson."

"Why didn't you just run away, Corrine?"

"Are you kidding? One doesn't run away from a pimp. That means more beatings—maybe even being killed. A pimp will always find his girl. I finally realized there was nothing I could do about it, so I just knuckled under."

Corrine could be submissive if she wanted to. But I sure wasn't going to be a prostitute, working for some filthy pimp—even a rich one. Never! So right then and there, I began to plan my escape!

8

That day, Corrine told me all about the weird world of prostitution. Don had made arrangements with his contacts at the hotels and other places to call the apartment, she said, and then the girls would go to the hotel room. We were supposed to charge as much as we could get, but never under one hundred dollars. Corrine tried to rationalize that we were high-class prostitutes—we didn't stand around on street corners propositioning. High class or no class, it made no difference to me. It was still prostitution, and I was determined I would have no part in it.

Corrine said the guys you had to go to bed with were called either "johns" or "tricks." I felt like calling them something else!

She also fouled up my escape plans when she told me that Don had instructed her to accompany me for a while. She was to stand outside my door, in case I got ideas of trying to run off.

That night they put me in a skin-tight dress—so tight it hurt. Once again Don threatened to beat me up if I tried to escape. Even Ribbons knew something was wrong. She didn't jump on me, just stayed close by my feet. It was too bad I couldn't take her with me. Maybe she'd fend off any perverted guy.

My first call came through about ten that night, from

a hotel on Fifty-sixth Street. The whole idea of prostitution had revolted me before. Now I was really scared—and queazy. It was about to happen!

Don went with Corrine and me. As he greeted the doorman, I wanted to scream to him to call the police and tell them I was being held as a slave.

The Rolls waited at the curb. Corrine opened the back door and motioned me in first. She sat there next to me, like a guard.

About six blocks from the apartment, Don turned his head. "Jackie," he said, "I've got something for you." He reached back, and I took a switchblade from his open hand!

"What do I need this for?" I asked in panic.

"Oh, just in case somebody tries to pull a fast one," he responded. "That thing will scare him to death."

I tried to push the switchblade back to Don. "Hey, listen, I don't know from square one about switchblades! I've never used one in my entire life. And I don't plan to start now!"

Corrine grabbed it just before it dropped to the floor. "Listen, Jackie," she said sternly, "you've got to know how to defend yourself. Sometimes guys get violent." She pushed the switchblade into my still-open hand.

"Let me tell you what goes on in a guy's head," she went on. "After he's been in bed with you, he thinks about his wife. That makes him feel guilty. So to get rid of his guilt, he'll turn on you. He rationalizes that you're the reason for his problem. That's when you've got to pull that switchblade. That'll bring the guy back to reality faster than anything. I know, Jackie, because it's happened to me. Chances are, it's likely to happen to you, too. You're going to need that blade."

I nodded and tucked it in my bra. Maybe she was right. Maybe someday I would need it. Maybe I could use it on Don Simpson!

When we pulled up in front of the hotel, the doorman came running over, opened the door, and stuck his head inside. I saw Don push something—it looked like money—into the doorman's hand. It was far more than a tip! I began to get the picture. Some guy in a hotel wanted a girl. He talked to the doorman. The doorman called Don. The doorman got a little something for his trouble! A lot of money must have been passed around.

The doorman snickered as he opened the door for us. "Have fun, girls!" he called.

I wanted to slap his face. Fun? This was absolutely horrible. And filthy.

Corrine must have anticipated my reaction because she quickly grabbed my right arm.

"Hey, listen," I said, pulling loose. "You don't need to worry about me. I'll obey. I'm smart enough for that."

She seemed relieved by my answer. Of course, I had no plan to knuckle under as she did and be a slave. I really had no plan at all, though. Maybe something would turn up so I could escape. But what?

We were alone in the elevator. She pushed the button for the fifteenth floor.

"What room are we going to?"

"Room 1526. There's a trick waiting for you."

My heart skipped a beat. What had previously been a disgusting idea was about to become a revolting reality!

At 1526 Corrine said, "A guy will answer. I'll stay out of sight here in the hallway for your protection."

"What do you mean, for my protection?" I asked sarcastically. "Why don't you go in and give the guy what he wants, and I'll stand here in the hallway."

"Come on now, Jackie," she answered. "Don't give me any trouble. Mr. Simpson told me that if you escaped from me, he was going to kill me! Then he will find you and kill you, too! So please play along, and both of us can stay alive. Okay?"

Now I was really in a jam. I was willing to take my chances to get away from Don Simpson. But could I face myself if I knew I was responsible for Corrine's death? She'd been pretty decent to me in the short time I'd known her.

When Corrine knocked, my heart went into my throat.

I heard the click. She stepped back against the wall where the guy couldn't see her. She didn't want to arouse his suspicions.

The guy peered out and then opened the door, smiling broadly. "Hey, come right in!" he said excitedly. He looked me over, like a customer examining a potential purchase. "Wow!" he drooled. "I didn't know I would be getting someone so young and beautiful. I mean, this is absolutely fantastic!"

I stepped inside, like a lamb to the slaughter. Corrine had already instructed me on my first duty—get the money.

In his eagerness, the guy was already taking off his undershirt. "Business before pleasure," I reminded him.

He reached for his wallet on the nightstand and asked, "How much?"

I blurted out, "One hundred dollars."

"One hundred dollars?" he remonstrated. "The doorman and I agreed on seventy-five dollars."

I had to think of something fast. "That was for an older woman," I said. "Standing before you is the best girl in town. My price is usually two hundred dollars. I'm giving you a real bargain. It's one hundred dollars, or I'm leaving."

He had gone too far to turn back now, so he pulled out five twenties and handed them to me. I stuffed them into my purse.

He was starting to take his pants off, and I knew what was expected of me next. I was supposed to undress.

What in the world was I going to do? Then I had an idea.

"Excuse me, sir. Let me step into your bathroom and prepare myself."

"Sure, honey. Help yourself."

I grabbed my purse and walked into the bathroom, locking the door behind me. I sat on the edge of the tub, lifted my dress, and started scratching upward on my leg onto my thighs. I dug harder and harder until the skin got really red and little specks of blood started to form under the skin. It was really hurting, but if it worked, it would hurt a lot less than what I was expected to do when I went back out there!

I opened the bathroom door and walked out. When he saw me still fully dressed, he looked puzzled. "Hey, I thought you said you were going to get ready," he protested. "What happened?"

I walked over toward him and said, "I've got this little problem. I'm sure it's nothing." I pulled my dress up a little above my knee, so he could see what I was talking about. "See this red rash? I just can't figure it out."

He stared at my leg. Then he looked at me. "Mister, that rash goes all the way up my leg," I said. "It's painful, too. What do you think it is?"

He bent over and started examining my leg. "And it really itches," I added.

"How long have you been prostituting?" he asked.

"Oh, about four years. I had to lay off for about six months not long ago because of venereal disease, but—"

He pulled away from me as though I had said I had leprosy. "Get out of here now, before I kill you!" he screamed. "No way am I going to get some disease from a slut like you!"

That was what I was hoping he would say, so I headed for the door. But before I got there, he grabbed my shoulder and spun me around. "Not so fast, slut!" he yelled. "Give me back my money!"

There was no way I could do that. I had to have that one hundred dollars to make Corrine and Don think I had gone through with the deal. But how could I fight him? Then I remembered the switchblade.

I quickly reached inside my bra and flicked the blade in front of his face. "Okay, mister, one little move on your part, and it's all over. Call the cops if you want to. But I'll tell them that I'm a prostitute and you're a trick. And they'll arrest both of us. That means you'll ride right along to jail with me. And mister, it's going to be in the papers. They're going to announce it on the radio. Is that what you want? I don't think so. So I'd advise you to just cool it and stand back."

His hands went above his head, and he backed away. I could tell from his eyes that he was scared to death. I was, too, but I was hoping it didn't show.

I unlocked the door and quickly stepped into the hall. Corrine fell in step alongside of me as we moved to the elevator.

"Wow, Jackie, that was quick!" she exclaimed. "I wish my customers were like that."

"Well, it was tough—and disgusting. But I gritted my teeth and made it through. I got one hundred dollars. Is that okay?"

"Good show! Mr. Simpson will be pleased."

As we exited from the hotel, we spotted the Rolls parked across the street. But Don was nowhere around. We crossed over and looked. Where was Don?

"That's strange," Corrine said. "He's always been right here waiting, before. He never lets us—or that Rolls—out of his sight."

"Now's our chance to escape from slavery," I said excitedly. "Let's run for it."

She laughed. "You've got to be kidding, Jackie. Where would you run to?"

I hadn't thought about that! Where could I go? If I went home, I'd get another beating—maybe even get killed. I guessed there really wasn't anywhere I could go.

But the whole idea fell apart at that moment, anyway, because Don emerged from a nearby bar. He and another guy walked up the street toward us. Both of them were gesturing excitedly.

As they got closer, I heard the guy say, "Okay, Don, I'll make you a deal you can't refuse. I'll give you ten thousand bucks."

"Do you have that kind of cash on you?" Don asked.

"Of course not, but I can get it right away. Is it a deal?"

"No way !" Don responded. Then he turned to us and said, "Jackie and Corrine, this is Victor Grames."

As Victor studied me, I noticed he was big and ugly.

"Jackie, Victor saw you get out of my car," Don explained, "and he wants to buy you for his stable. He says he really needs a young one to work for him."

I stepped back in shock. They were bargaining for me! Would Don sell me for ten thousand dollars?

"Listen Don, I really need her," Victor was saying. "She's young. She's beautiful. She can make better money for me with my clientele. So let's make a deal."

Don pushed away Victor's offered hand and said, "Absolutely no way. Not for ten thousand dollars." With that, he unlocked the car door and ordered both of us inside. "I'll be with you in a minute," he said.

Don shut the door and walked a few steps away. I wanted to put down the window to hear what they were saying, but Corrine told me that would be a good way to get Don mad at me. But I could see them arguing back and forth, haggling over how much I was worth. How absolutely degrading!

"Who is this Victor?" I asked.

"You don't know Victor?"

"No, I don't know Victor. This whole business is new to me."

"Well, Victor is somebody you don't want to know. He's the meanest dude in Times Square."

"Well, he certainly looks mean," I said. "You don't think Don would sell me to him, do you?"

"Don Simpson might do anything," Corrine told me. "If I were you, I'd offer a little prayer that he didn't sell me to Victor. That dude sets his girls up with the worst filth—perverts, bums, anybody with any money at all. I mean the guy has absolutely no standards of any kind. He is the worst!"

Now I was in for it. If I had to go with Victor, that would be the end of my life for sure.

Knowing that my future rested on the outcome of their decision, I leaned forward and watched intently. They were still flailing their arms wildly. Finally they stopped and shook hands. Oh, no! They had made a deal.

Don walked back to the car. I expected him to open the back door and order me to go with Victor. But instead, he just opened his door and got in behind the wheel.

"Jackie," he said as he shut his door, started the engine, and glided out into the flow of traffic, "I've decided that you're too valuable for me to sell right now. Victor really wanted you. I've never seen him get so excited about a girl. But I really want to see how you work out. I can always sell you to Victor if you give me too much trouble!"

He looked over his shoulder to see if I had gotten the message. I had.

Back at the apartment, I gave Don the one hundred dollars, and he headed for his bedroom. Corrine whispered to me that he had his safe in there. Only he knew the combination.

We sat around the living room, drinking coffee. Nobody said much. When the phone rang, I jumped. Would I have to go again? Would the same trick work?

Don wrote down the name of the hotel and the room number. When he hung up, he said, "The guy wants Juanita. He had her last week when he was in town."

"Do you mind if I go to my bedroom?" I asked Don. "If a call comes, you can get me."

"Yes, I guess that's okay. Just don't get your hair messed up."

When I opened the door to my room, Ribbons jumped all over me. She was so glad to see me. I flopped onto the bed, and she snuggled in my arms. She seemed to sense that I was deeply troubled and started to lick my arms. Tears welled up in my eyes as I realized that she was the only one who really loved me, the only one who cared what happened to me.

I lay there thinking about the horrible mess I had gotten myself into. Sure, I lived in luxury. But to what purpose? I was a slave! I had no rights. I couldn't come and go as I pleased. Now I didn't even control my own body!

I looked down at Ribbons, now sleeping peacefully in my arms. If I did get away, I couldn't leave her behind. Don would probably kill her to get even with me.

I went to my closet and got out my biggest purse—a cloth one I had purchased while I was still the favored "daughter." Ribbons trotted over after me, and I picked her up and set her in the purse. She fit perfectly!

Before I could take her out again, someone knocked on my door. "We got a call, Jackie," Corrine's voice told me. "Let's go. Don doesn't want to keep a john waiting."

I dumped the stuff from my other purse in on top of Ribbons and even stuck in four dog biscuits. I was hoping they would keep her quiet. If she barked, I'd really be in trouble!

I heard Don screaming from the apartment door, "Hurry up, Jackie!"

This time he drove us over to a beautiful hotel near the United Nations building. Once again, he paid off the doorman.

When Corrine and I were walking through the lobby toward the elevator, she asked me, "How come you brought your dog along?"

Her question startled me, but I didn't show any reaction. "What are you talking about?"

She pointed toward my purse. "All the time we were in the car, I watched your purse. The first time I saw it moving, I almost came out of my skin. Then I realized what you had done. You really like that dog, don't you?"

"Ribbons is the only true friend I've got," I told her. "I mean, the *only* one."

"Well, you sure took an awful chance by bringing her, Jackie. Suppose the dog started barking and putting up a big fuss. If we had to turn around and go back to the apartment because of that, Don would kill that dog. And he might kill you, too. You see, sometimes guys who call get really impatient. If the girl doesn't show up right away, they might call someone else. So if you had been responsible for missing this appointment, Don would have slapped you silly. I know he would take your dog away. That man really can get violent, Jackie. You haven't seen him at his worst. So don't ever try this again!"

I sure didn't want to be responsible for Ribbons' getting hurt or killed. But if I escaped, I sure wanted to have her with me.

"Okay, this was just a little lark," I told Corrine. "I promise I won't do it again."

This time it was room 626. When we stopped before the door, I waited for Corrine to knock. Instead, she opened her purse, pulled out a screwdriver, and started unscrewing the numbers on the door.

"What on earth are you doing?" I asked in amazement.

"Don warned me this might be a setup," she said. "So I'm changing this room number. It's going to be 662 now."

"What do you mean, a setup?"

"Well, a guy who's really a cop will call Don up and ask for a girl. After she goes inside, the door will come flying open, and a bunch of cops will come storming in to arrest her. So by changing the numbers, I'm giving us a fighting chance. If someone comes looking for 626, I'll be standing here by 662 and tell them it's on the other side of the elevators. That will put them off long enough to give us a chance to escape."

It seemed like a stupid idea to me. The cops would be able to spot a room between 624 and 628 and know it wasn't 662! I thought what she meant was that it would give *her* time to escape! But there wasn't any point in arguing. She already had the numbers changed.

She knocked and stepped back. This time a foreign-looking man with a thin moustache answered.

I walked in and shut the door. Should I try the venereal-disease route again? It had worked for me before, so it seemed like my best shot.

The guy still hadn't said anything. He just started unbuttoning his shirt.

"Business before pleasure," I said.

He shrugged. I said it again: "Business before pleasure."

"No speakee Englass," he responded.

Good grief! Corrine hadn't prepared me for this! I was going to have to show him some money.

"Money," I said, pointing to my purse. He reached for his wallet.

"One hundred dollars," I told him.

He shrugged again, so I took his wallet, counted out one hundred dollars and handed the wallet back to him. He smiled and nodded. I realized then I could have taken more, and he would never have known the difference.

"I'm going into the bathroom," I said. "I want to look real pretty for you."

He shrugged again. He had no idea what I was saying.

I guessed it didn't make any difference. I just went into the bathroom and started scratching my legs again. They were still sore from what I had done to them a few hours before, but I gritted my teeth and kept at it. I had to make this look good.

When I opened the bathroom door, I pulled up my dress, pointed to my leg, and said, "I have a bad case of venereal disease."

He bent over, studied my leg, straightened up, and went on taking off his clothes. Now what was I going to do? He hadn't understood a word I said.

I glanced upward. That's when I noticed it—a smoke detector. A plan started to form in my mind.

"I'm going to make this really exotic," I said. "Why don't we get some smoke in here? You know, the way they probably do in your country. It will smell nice."

He smiled and nodded, but I knew he didn't understand.

I found a book of matches in an ashtray, lit one, and held it high over my head, as close to the smoke detector as I could. Then I tried to do a little dance. He seemed pleased.

I lit a few more matches, but nothing happened. I had to have more smoke. So I tried two matches at a time. Then three at a time. Still nothing.

I went back into the bathroom and made a torch out of some toilet paper. I lit it and held it over my head as I danced. That did it. The alarm screamed in the hallway.

The toilet paper was about to burn my fingers, so I dashed it into the toilet. I heard people out in the hall yelling, "Fire! Fire! Fire!"

The foreigner looked at me. I didn't have to explain to him what was happening. He started running around excitedly, looking for his clothes. It was almost comical to see the guy trying to get them on. I thought about offering to help him, but I didn't want him to get dressed too soon. That would foul up part of my plan.

Then I heard the sirens out in the street and knew the fire trucks had arrived. I waited, hoping Corrine wouldn't try to break in and "save" me.

Finally, I heard firemen in the hall checking the rooms. When I figured they were just about at this door, I ran out into the hall. Good! No Corrine! I had my purse with Ribbons inside, and I had the one hundred dollars, too. As a fireman headed toward me, I yelled, "What's the quickest way out?"

He pointed down the hall. "Out that exit. And hurry!"

I ran toward it. Everybody else was running down the stairs, fleeing for their lives. I ran up six flights, struggling against the people coming down.

On the twelfth floor, I ran down a hallway. In their rush to exit, people had left their doors open. I picked a room, went in, and locked the door behind me.

I flopped into a chair, opened my purse, and out jumped Ribbons, her tail wagging.

So far so good. But I knew that in a few minutes, whoever was occupying this room would be coming back. What was I going to say?

9

I had had presence of mind enough to pick a room facing the street, so I walked over to the window and looked down. Amid the five fire engines and all the confusion, I spotted the familiar Rolls Royce, with a man and a woman standing next to it. It must be Don and Corrine, carefully studying the crowd and the exits. I knew what they were looking for—me!

I noticed Don looking up, and I ducked back. I didn't think he could see me at that distance, but any figure looking out of a window would be suspicious when the hotel was supposed to be totally evacuated.

I settled back into an easy chair, wondering what my next move ought to be. A few minutes later, someone knocked on the door. Oh, no! Had Don seen me at the window?

"Is anybody in there?" a voice called.

I clapped my hand over Ribbons' mouth. I hoped he was only checking to be sure everybody was out. I waited, hardly daring to breathe, until finally I heard footsteps moving away and down the hall. Whoever that was wasn't going to bother me. But what about when all the guests were allowed back into the hotel? I really felt trapped. If I tried to escape, Don would be waiting for me, and he'd probably kill me for what I'd done. Even if I did get away, I knew he'd hunt me down. But I was sure going to give it a try. I'd make it difficult for him.

After all the excitement had died down, the moment I dreaded arrived. I heard the doorknob rattle. The door opened, and there stood a man. He stared at me in surprise, then backed out, saying, "I'm sorry. I must have the wrong room."

A few minutes later, I heard the doorknob rattle again. The same man opened the door and said, "I'm sorry, ma'am, but I think you must have the wrong room."

"Oh, no!" I responded indignantly. "I've been in this room for several days now. Just me and my dog."

Walking in and looking around, the man said, "Look, lady. I don't know what your game is, but this is my room! Look over in that corner. Those are men's shoes—and they're mine! Look—here's my room key. It says 1243. That's the number on the door. What's your room number?"

"Oh, is this 1243?" I asked lamely. "You're right. This isn't my room. I'm supposed to be in 1248. I guess with all the excitement, I got mixed up."

With that, I headed out the door with Ribbons. As I went down the hall, a man got off the elevator, looked at me, and did a double take. "Hey, little girl," he said, "are you lost?"

I shook my head, but he went on anyway: "I was just on the elevator with some guy who can't find his daughter. Seems they got separated in all the excitement. He described her, and you fit the description. He got off on the sixth floor. . . ." His voice trailed off. Then he continued, "Are you sure you're not his daughter? He sure seemed upset!"

I got the message. Don Simpson was roaming these halls looking for me. He wouldn't give up!

I followed the man down the hall and waited until he opened his door. Then I pushed past him. He followed me in, but left the door open. "What's going on?" he demanded.

I moved behind him and locked the door. Then I set Ribbons down and started unbuttoning my blouse. "Whatever are you doing?" he demanded.

I didn't say a word. By this time, I had taken my blouse off and was starting to unzip my skirt. I kept hoping it would work, because I sure didn't want to get completely undressed in front of the guy.

As he watched me fumbling with my zipper, he yelled, "Young lady, stop! Don't you dare take off your clothes in front of me! I'll have you know I'm a happily married man with three children of my own. I don't do this kind of thing. Why, I'm old enough to be your father. I ought to turn you over my knee and wallop you good."

I stopped tugging and said, "Okay, mister, do you know why that guy is trying to find me? Because what you told me was a signal. He knows I'll be in your room. You see, mister, this is a setup, and you have just been set up!"

"I've been what? What are you talking about?"

"This is how it works," I explained. "He'll give me time to get my clothes off. Then he'll come barging in and find me here with you. You know what it's going to look like. The next thing he will do is pull out a badge. Then you're supposed to get scared when he tells you to come along with him to the police station. Of course, you don't want to go there. You don't want to be accused, either falsely or otherwise, of having a prostitute in your room. You won't be able to face the bad publicity. It might even wreck your marriage. So you offer to pay him if he'll let you off the hook. And you're going to pay dearly. That's what I mean—you've been set up."

I watched his expression, hoping he would believe me. If he'd been around New York City before, he would know it wasn't all that farfetched.

"He really wouldn't do anything like that, would he?"

"Hey, mister," I responded, "he'll even kill you if you resist. He's armed with a .45 automatic. So you're going to pay—one way or another."

He didn't seem to be overly frightened by that. He just looked me straight in the eye and asked, "Young lady, why are you telling me all this?"

"Because I like you," I answered. "You seem like a decent chap. But more than that, I want out of this filthy trap I'm in. I want to get away from that filthy pimp. I thought maybe if I warned you about what he is planning to do, you could help me escape from his clutches."

"Well," he said, "put your blouse back on, and we'll talk about it."

I quickly slipped the blouse on, and he said gallantly, "And now, damsel in distress, what can I do to help you?"

All this time I had been concocting my scheme. Would it work? We had to try.

"All right," I said, "here's what we're going to do. You call the hotel security guard. Tell him your daughter has just had an epileptic seizure and you have to rush her to the hospital. You need his help getting her to a taxi. When the guard comes up, I'll be on the floor, faking it. You tell him to put his handcuffs on me to protect me from injuring myself. Then the two of you take me downstairs, and we get into a taxi and drive off. I'm hoping my pimp will see the guard and the handcuffs and figure I've been busted. He'll figure you are an undercover cop."

"I don't know if I should really get into something like this," he said, rubbing his chin thoughtfully. "I just hope you're not telling me some big story or that this is not some sorority prank."

"Hey, mister, I'm telling you the honest truth!" I told him. "If my pimp gets us, it'll be all over for me—and for you, too. You've got to help me."

He still didn't seem convinced and said, "I think I'll just call the security guard and have you thrown out of my room."

"Okay mister, I hate to do this, but you leave me no choice," I said as I ran over and grabbed the doorknob. I'm going to open this door and yell. That's the signal for my pimp, Don Simpson, to come running. And when he comes through this door, everything is going to pop. He'll rob you. He'll pistol-whip you. He may even kill you. And I'm not kidding!"

The guy looked as though he could take care of himself in a fair fight. But what I was describing was hardly fair, and he began to look a little worried.

"Okay, okay, I'll go along with you. But so help me, if I get into trouble with the law over this, I'm going to kill both you and your pimp!"

With that, he walked over to the telephone, dialed the operator, and asked for security. He explained to the guard what the problem was.

A few minutes after he hung up, I got down on the floor, ready to go into my act when I heard someone knock on the door. As I lay there, I said, "Now don't forget the handcuffs. And don't forget I'm your daughter. By the way, what's your name?"

"Oh, no, you don't!" he responded. "There's no way I'm going to give you my name. If this is a frame-up, you'll never know who I am."

"For crying out loud, quit being so scared," I told him. "My name is Jackie Marshall. Let's call you Bernard Sullivan. That will make me Jackie Sullivan, your daughter. Okay?"

He nodded. I repeated the name to myself several times. Then in a few minutes, we heard that anticipated knock and the call, "Security."

I began to shake. I drew saliva and pushed it to the

side of my mouth so it would run down my face. I jerked and twitched.

The man unlocked the door and said to the guard, "My, I'm so glad you could come so quickly, sir. This is terrible. My daughter and I have been in town waiting to see a specialist about her condition. She has an appointment tomorrow, but she started having this convulsion. I don't dare wait until tomorrow. I think I'd better get her to a hospital right away."

One thing for sure: I had picked a good liar!

The security guard bent over me, and I really put on an act.

"Wow, she looks in bad shape!" he said. "I'll call an ambulance right away."

"Oh, no!" the man protested. "There isn't time for that. You know how long it could take an ambulance to get here! The best thing is for you to help me get her to a taxi, and I'll rush her there myself."

"Yes, that sounds like a good idea," the guard said. "But how are we going to get her downstairs?"

"Well, first thing," the man said, "I want you to put your handcuffs on her. You noticed how she twitches around. She's been known to really hurt herself. The handcuffs will be for her own protection."

I jerked some more and could sense the security guard bending over me, pushing my arms together, and then—*click!* Everything was working exactly according to plan! But I sure felt trapped!

"We can ease her to her feet," the man explained. The two of them gently lifted me. Then Ribbons started barking at them.

"Hey, little dog, you'll be okay," the guard told her gently.

As we walked out the door, Ribbons came running after us. "Do you want me to take care of the dog while you go to the hospital?" the guard asked.

I tried to shake my head no. "Young lady, do you want the dog with you?"

I nodded. "I'm sure it'll be all right if you take him, sir," he said. "Maybe the dog will help calm her down."

When the elevator stopped on the first floor, I knew I was about to face my moment of truth. Sure enough, when we walked through the lobby, there stood Don and Corrine. Don started over, but I spun around so he could see the handcuffs. As I spun, the two men grappled with me. It really looked authentic!

When I turned and looked again, Don had backed off and was heading for his car. I'm sure he thought the man was a detective, especially because the security guard accompanied us.

A taxi pulled up at the guard's signal. In a moment I would be out of there and away from the dreadful Don Simpson. Then I had a horrifying thought. Would the man have enough sense to get the key to the handcuffs? I'd better not take a chance.

I snapped my head forward, then backward. I stared at the security guard who was standing next to me and asked, as though I were just coming out of a daze, "Where am I?"

Then I turned and, putting a note of fright in my voice, said, "Dad! Dad! Where am I? What's happened?"

"It's okay, Jackie," he responded. "Everything is going to be okay. We're just taking you to the hospital to get some medication. Everything will be just fine."

I struggled, trying to get lose from the handcuffs. I knew I couldn't get free, but I needed to set the stage for me to say, "Something seems to be the matter with my hands. I can't get them from behind my back."

"We've got handcuffs on you, Jackie," Mr. Sullivan said. "I didn't want you to hurt yourself."

I glanced down the street to where Don was standing

by his car with Corrine. He was far enough away that I was sure he couldn't tell what we were talking about. I didn't want these guys to undo the handcuffs now. That could blow the whole thing. But I had to have that key.

"Did I go into a convulsion and hurt myself again?"

"No, not this time. We got the handcuffs on before you got too violent."

"Oh, good!" I responded. "I'm glad you did that, Dad. Maybe we should buy a pair. It might save me a lot of bruises."

"I'd like to let you have mine," the guard said, "but I'm not allowed to do that. Maybe I could make arrangements to get a set for you, though."

"Dad, I'm worried that I might have another convulsion in the taxi on the way to the hospital," I said. "Maybe you'd better keep these on me."

Mr. Sullivan turned to the guard and asked, "Do you mind if we borrow them for a little while? I'm sure we'll be back before long, and I'll make sure you get them."

"Sure, that's okay," the guard said. "Just as long as you make sure I get them back."

"Make sure you bring along the key, Dad," I chuckled.

The guard reached into his pocket and pulled out the key, handing it to Mr. Sullivan. And I breathed a sigh of relief.

The guard also told the driver where to take us, and we were on our way. I was overjoyed at how successfully our little ruse had worked.

I looked back, wondering what Don would do now. That's when I spotted that familiar Rolls about a half a block behind us.

"We're in trouble!" I whispered to Mr. Sullivan. "That filthy pimp is following us. We've got to think of something else."

He glanced back. "You mean that guy in the Rolls?"

"Yes, he's the one."

"Well, you got me into this," he said, "so you'd better think of something else."

We couldn't go to the hospital. Don would walk right in and grab me. But he wouldn't follow me into a police station! He'd get a lawyer to get me out of that kind of a jam; he wouldn't go there himself! That had to be the answer. We'd go to the police station!

But what could I tell the police? Certainly not that I was a prostitute. They'd lock me up for that, and probably use me to try to get Don Simpson. Then my life wouldn't be worth a nickel.

"Tell the taxi driver to take us to the nearest police station," I whispered. "It's our only way out."

"Yes, I think you're right," Mr. Sullivan responded. "I sure don't want to do battle with any pimp."

Mr. Sullivan told the driver to take us to the police station. I guess that didn't surprise the driver too much—he had seen the handcuffs. We turned several corners. Don Simpson stayed right on our tail.

"I've been thinking about what we're going to tell the police," I whispered. "I'm sure that our walking in there will shake my pimp. And you can tell the cops that you were playing a game with your daughter and you lost the key to the handcuffs. Tell them you had the key in your lap, but when you stood up, you couldn't find it anywhere. Now just stick the key in your pants cuff. While you're telling them the story, just sort of reach down there and 'discover' it."

"Jackie, I'm getting deeper and deeper into this thing. So help me, if this doesn't work, you're going to pay, and pay dearly. What I really ought to do is turn you over to the police when we get there."

I got mad and snarled, "Okay, why don't you do that? But when they look up my record and discover I've been busted for prostitution a number of times, there's no way they are going to believe you—especially when I tell them you propositioned me and wouldn't pay me. After that, I'll tell them you're a pervert and that you handcuffed me. You'll have a tough time explaining that one. They'll believe me because of my record."

"Okay, okay, you've got me over a barrel. I'll go through with it. Just calm down."

"Put that key in your pants cuff," I whispered. "And make sure you don't lose it when we get out of the cab."

A few minutes later, the driver announced that we were at the police station. Mr. Sullivan paid, and we got out onto the curb. No sooner had the taxi driven off than Don and Corrine drove up beside us.

"What happened, Jackie?" Corrine asked through her open window.

I spun around and screamed, "What do you think happened? It was a setup, just as you said. I got busted!"

As soon as he heard *busted,* Don took off like I'd never seen him drive before. I mean, his tires screeched so loud you could have heard them over in Jersey! He even streaked through a red light!

Cops were coming and going all over the place. One of them walked up when he saw us and asked, "What have we here?"

I held my breath. Would he still go along?

"Oh, my daughter and I were playing a little game," Mr. Sullivan said. "I got her handcuffed, and I seem to have lost the key."

"Well, come on in," the cop said. "We can take a hammer and chisel and get them off."

The cop grabbed my arm and escorted us inside. The sergeant at the desk asked, "O'Reilly, what do you have there?"

O'Reilly laughed. "It's a father-daughter deal. No arrest. The father put handcuffs on the daughter and then lost the key."

The sergeant laughed, and Mr. Sullivan explained, "I got these handcuffs as a gag gift. You see, I'm a salesman. My friends said that a salesman, if he's handcuffed, will be able to keep his hands to himself while he's on the road. I guess you know what they mean?"

The officers roared. I'll tell you, this Sullivan was a great liar.

"Well, I was fooling around and put the cuffs on my daughter Jackie. I had the key right in my lap. But when I stood up to take them off, I couldn't find that stupid key anywhere. We looked all over—on the floor, in the chair, everywhere. I can't imagine what happened to it. I know we must have spent over an hour looking for it. Oh, dear, this is so embarrassing. . . ." His voice trailed off.

"Could it have slipped into your pants or shoes?" the cop asked.

Mr. Sullivan pulled out his pockets. He was really playing the game. Then he reached down his pant leg, into his cuff. A look of shock and triumph crossed his face as he grabbed the key and raised it high. "Would you believe that here it is? It got caught in my cuff!"

"Well, mister, I think we ought to put your daughter in jail for all the trouble she's caused you," the sergeant said.

Quite a few policemen had gathered around us by this time, and they all thought the whole thing was terribly funny. I really didn't, but I knew I'd better laugh.

"Oh, I'm so embarrassed," Mr. Sullivan said. "This is terrible."

"Think nothing of it," the sergeant said. "It's just a good thing you found that key. I'd hate to break those handcuffs. They look like a pretty good pair."

I was hoping Mr. Sullivan wouldn't blurt out that he had gotten them from a security guard. But he played the game all the way down the line. He just reached over, unlocked the cuffs, and stuck them into his pocket.

"Oh, Daddy, I'm so relieved!" I said, as I threw my arms around him. "I was absolutely scared to death."

Then I felt something tugging at my shoe. I looked down, and there was Ribbons. It was a good thing she had kept track of me, because I'd almost forgotten her in all the excitement. I guess she just followed along wherever I went.

My plan had worked perfectly, but I knew I needed to get out of there quickly, before Don Simpson or his lawyer showed up. I didn't want to blow my escape at this point.

"Come on, Daddy," I said, grabbing Mr. Sullivan's arm. "Let's go back to our hotel. This time I'll put the cuffs on you!"

Everybody laughed again. At least we had provided a comic relief for the police that night.

As we went out the door, I quickly looked both ways. I couldn't see any sign of Don Simpson.

Then I turned toward Mr. Sullivan. "I don't really know who you are, sir," I said, "but I want to tell you that you just saved my life. I don't know how to thank you. You're such a great guy. I wish you really were my father."

His face flushed. He could easily have taken advantage of me a couple of times, but he didn't. He must have been a good man, a decent man. And I loved him for that.

"Well, Jackie, I almost hate to see this end," he told me. "I can't believe I could have gotten involved in something like this. I'm usually considered quite an old stick-in-the-mud. This is the most exciting thing that's happened to me in years!"

I stood there looking at him, hardly knowing what to say or do next. So I just threw my arms around him and broke down. I felt his arms go around me. It was the first time I had ever experienced having a man's arms around me and not being afraid. Yet Mr. Sullivan was a stranger!

"Now, now, Jackie," he comforted, "everything will be all right. Is there anything else I can do for you?"

I drew back. "I'm sorry, Mr. Sullivan. I guess I was just overcome with emotion. You saved me from that horrible pimp, and I sort of owe my life to you. Thanks ever so much."

"Now, Jackie, it was really nothing. I was just glad to help you out."

"Nothing?" I echoed. "You risked your life for me. I'll never forget it. Thanks, Dad. And good-bye. I love you."

I had to bite my tongue to keep from going to pieces again. I wondered what it would be like to really love your father.

I started to pull away, but he hugged me again. "Good-bye, daughter. And I love you, too."

I felt so loved, so secure in his arms. But I knew I had to get away from there as fast as I could. I drew back and looked up into his face. Tears were trickling down his cheeks. I couldn't believe it. He was a total stranger, yet he really seemed to love me and be concerned about me. I guessed there must be love in this world. But would I ever find it?

I spun around and headed for the subway, Ribbons at my heels. I knew I had to move quickly.

But the question Corrine had asked me earlier haunted me now. Where could I go? There was no place I'd be safe. But I sure had to get away from Don Simpson now. He'd probably beat me to death if he caught up with me. And for all I knew, that Rolls Royce might be cruising these streets right now, waiting and watching for me. So I started to run.

10

I kept glancing around as I hurried toward the subway station. I had just about decided that the only thing I could do was to go back home. Maybe Mom had decided to leave Dad, and that would provide a bearable existence for me with her. This business of running away sure wasn't all it was cracked up to be. If I could work out something at home, never again would I run away. Never again would I steal or use drugs. I was going to be a totally new person.

Suddenly a pusher appeared right in front of me. "Hey, baby, want to buy some good stuff?" he asked. "I just got a shipment in from Turkey. I mean, I have the best stuff in town."

All my resolutions vanished like an ice cube in the hot sun when this opportunity presented itself. It had been awhile since I'd done drugs, and they seemed especially appealing right about now. After the harrowing experience I had just been through, I sure could use something to calm my nerves.

"How much for a couple of bags?"

"Forty bucks."

Ribbons snarled at the guy from the safety of my arms. She probably would have made a good cop. She didn't have any use for guys who were up to no good.

"Hey, Ribbons, calm down," I said. "This guy's not going to hurt you."

The pusher reached over to pet her, but Ribbons bared her teeth and snarled and snapped.

"Hey, that's a pretty brave dog for being so little," he said, jerking his hand back to safety. "Want to sell him?"

"Well, first of all she's not a him," I said. "And second of all, she's not for sale."

"Not even for ten bags of dope?"

"Not for any price. She's the only friend I've got."

The pusher laughed. "Hey, baby, you have a friend. It's called dope. That's a friend that will bring you up every time!"

I wasn't amused. I knew dope was no friend. I knew a person could get hooked. It hadn't hooked me yet, but I was finding it harder and harder to stay away from it. It sure wasn't as good a friend as Ribbons.

I hugged my little poodle tightly as she snuggled against my chest. I guess we needed each other.

I handed the pusher two twenties as he handed me two bags.

"Do you know where I can get a set of works?" I asked him.

"Sure do, babe. Just down that alley, behind a couple of garbage cans, I've got a set stashed."

"How much to use your works?"

"Twenty-five bucks."

"Twenty-five bucks? That's robbery!"

"Hey, babe, as I say, I have a set of works available for twenty-five bucks. It's no skin off my nose whether you use it or not. If you don't want to pay twenty-five dollars, then forget it."

"Hey, man, don't get so upset," I responded. "I was just trying to work a deal."

"The only deal is twenty-five bucks," he said firmly.

I handed him two more twenties. He pulled out a wad of money and handed me back a ten and a five.

"Wow! You sure have a lot of money!" I exclaimed. "Business must be pretty good!"

"Yes, it is. That's because I have good stuff. Do you want to work for me?"

I stepped back. "No way am I going to work for another pimp!" I protested.

"Hey, babe, I ought to slap you across the face!" he shouted. "I wasn't talking about prostituting and pimping. I can't stand pimps. I have a kid sister who got trapped by one of those filthy scum. She works like a slave. He gives her nothing and he slaps her around."

"I know what that's all about," I told him.

"What I mean is that you could sell dope for me. We could form a partnership."

I knew better than to get into that kind of mess. In New York you could get a life sentence for being a pusher. A prostitution charge meant fifteen days if you got a mean judge. No way was I going to get into drug sales and get sent up for life!

I decided I'd better get away from him quickly. I knew better than to do what he was suggesting, but all that money was looking more and more tempting!

"Okay, where are those works?" I asked.

"Follow me."

We walked on down the street, making small talk, and took a few steps into an alley. "Look down there," he said, pointing. "See that huge cardboard box? Right behind it you'll find a garbage can. Beside it you'll see a smaller box. Push it out of the way, and you'll find a loose brick. Pull it out, and right there is my set of works. You'll even find some water and matches in the box. Got it?"

A little red flag went up in my brain. I knew what was

going to happen. As soon as I walked down there, he was going to disappear, and I'd discover—nothing! Smart guy. But not smart enough for me!

"Hey, do you really think I'm from the country?" I asked. "You know, and I know, that there are no works down there. So give me back my twenty-five dollars!"

He stiffened. "I ought to bust you right in the mouth," he snarled. "Come on!"

Grabbing me by the arm, he pulled me down the alley. He was so mad that he kicked the big box clear across the alley. He shoved the other box out of the way, pulled out the brick, reached inside, and pulled out the set of works.

I was glad it was dark so he couldn't see my red face. "Hey, mister, I'm sorry!" I said over and over. "You know how it is. Never trust a junkie. Never trust a pimp. I figured you couldn't trust a pusher. I guess I was wrong."

"Okay, forget it," he said, a little calmer now. "Go ahead and use the set and put it back. If you try to steal it, I'll kill you!"

I took the set of works and knelt beside the big box, while he made his way back down the alley. I loaded the needle with both bags, fleetingly wondering whether that would be too much after all this time.

As I applied the tourniquet and started to put the needle into my armpit, Ribbons snarled. I guess she knew that what I was doing was wrong.

I didn't care, for I felt the rush immediately. Then I felt my head spinning. I had overdosed!

When you overdose, nothing happens. You don't dream. You don't feel anything. Nothing happens—except death.

In the distance, I heard Ribbons barking. I tried to open my eyes to check on her, but I couldn't force them to open. Then the barking sounded farther away, as though it were coming from a hollow chamber. Then it became clearer. I heard a voice saying, "She's coming to!"

I fluttered my eyelids and finally forced my eyes open. I was staring into the face of a policeman!

I realized I was stretched out flat in that stinking alley. In fact, I was lying in some garbage! I tried to sit up, but I couldn't. It felt as though every last ounce of strength had ebbed from my body.

"What happened?" I asked weakly.

"What do you mean, what happened?" the officer replied in surprise. "You know what happened. You just overdosed, young lady. You're mighty lucky to be alive!"

I looked around and noticed Ribbons prancing all over the place, happy I had come to.

"How did you find me?" I asked the cop.

"Well, it was a pretty strange coincidence," he said. "An old lady up in one of these tenements was awakened because of a dog barking. She got up to yell at it, but the dog wouldn't stop. She told us she could make out what looked like a human form near where the dog was standing, so she called us. I don't know whose dog this is, but you can thank him for saving your life! It wouldn't have been very long before you had stopped breathing!"

My befuddled mind was clearing enough that I remembered what that stupid pusher had said about dope being my friend. Some friend! It had almost killed me. I was right in my assessment that Ribbons was my only real friend!

She was snuggled up next to me again, every once in a while turning to try to lick my face.

"I've called an ambulance," the cop said. "We're going to have to take you to a hospital."

I protested that I didn't want to go, but I was so weak

that I was just about resigned to the idea.

I heard the siren getting closer and closer. Then the ambulance stopped at the entrance to the alley. Two attendants jumped out and came running with a stretcher. They gently lifted me onto it, strapped me on, and started carrying me away.

"My dog!" I yelled. "Grab my dog!"

"Sorry, lady, but we can't take a dog in the ambulance," one attendant replied. "It's against regulations. Besides, they wouldn't let you keep him at the hospital."

"I'll take care of your dog," the cop said. "I'll take him over to the pound."

"No! No!" I screamed. "I can't take a chance on what might happen to her over there!"

Everybody was ignoring my requests, and the two guys were about to push me into the ambulance.

"Let me down!" I screamed. "I'm nineteen years old, and if you take me to the hospital against my will, I'm going to sue both of you! I'm going to sue the hospital, I'm going to sue the doctors, and I'm going to sue this cop!"

"You refuse to go to the hospital?" one of the attendants asked.

I let out an oath and added, "I sure do. Put me down!"

They unstrapped me, and one of them ordered, "Okay, get off!" I rolled over and gingerly set my feet on the ground. My legs buckled. The officer gently helped me up.

"Listen, you really need to go to the hospital," he said. "Why don't you—"

"Cop, you know what my dog did," I interrupted. "She saved my life. I'm not going to go anywhere without her!"

The ambulance driver was thoroughly disgusted with the whole scene. "Listen, lady," he said sharply, "we don't have time to play games with dogs. If you want us to, we'll take you. If not, we're moving on. We've got more to do than to stand here and argue with some stupid junkie!"

I clenched my fist and was about to let that character have it, but I couldn't even raise my arm. I had no strength.

The cop was a little more sympathetic. I guess he could understand how I felt about Ribbons. So he said, "Fellows, she doesn't have to go to the hospital if she doesn't want to go. I'll take care of her."

The two attendants jammed the stretcher back in the ambulance and took off as though they were mad at the whole world.

That was close! I turned to the cop, and he helped me over to a place where I could lean against a building. "Thank you, sir," I told him. "I appreciate your being so understanding of my predicament. Now I guess I'd better be on my way."

"Not so fast," the cop said sternly. 'We've got a little problem we have to deal with first. What is this?"

He held out his hand. In it was a set of works.

"Those aren't mine," I protested.

"Of course they're not yours!" he answered sarcastically. "I suppose they just dropped down from the sky and landed in your arm. Listen, young lady, when I ran up to where you were, I found these works stuck in your arm."

"That may be so," I said, "but they're really not mine. They belong to a pusher."

"Sure, sure. They belong to a pusher. But young lady, let me tell you again that I found them in *your* arm. I didn't find them in some pusher's arm. So as far as I am concerned, they belong to *you.* And that means you're under arrest for possession of a hypodermic needle."

"What?" I exploded.

"Let me read you your rights."

He pulled out a little card and began reading. Among the things he read was that I didn't have to say one more thing until I consulted a lawyer.

He put the card away and said, "You'll have to come along with me." He grabbed my arm to lead me back to the street. I started to jerk away, but before I knew what was happening, he had spun me around and clicked his handcuffs on me. That was the second time that night I had had handcuffs on, only this time I didn't have access to the key!

When the cop handcuffed me, Ribbons started snapping at him. He ignored her and started moving me toward his car.

"What about my dog?" I asked.

"Listen," the cop replied, "you're the only one I'm busting. As far as I'm concerned, the dog is innocent. She had no hypodermic needle. Besides, we don't have jails for dogs. She is free to go."

"Please, officer, please," I begged, ignoring his sarcasm. "Please let me take Ribbons with me. She's the only friend I've got in this whole world."

"Listen, young lady, I'd like to help you out. But we've got regulations. We can't have dogs in jail!"

I had to think of something, and I blurted out, "Officer, I'll make a deal with you. If you let me take my dog with me, I'll put the finger on the pusher. After all, he's the guy you really ought to be busting."

He stopped. "Are you positive you want to work with us?"

"Absolutely, provided we make a deal about my dog. I just can't leave her here on the streets. Somebody will steal her. Besides—"

"I know," the officer interrupted, "she saved your life. Well, I don't know what we can do. But we'll try. And you'd better not welsh on the deal!"

When the cop picked up Ribbons, she stopped her

barking and sort of snuggled next to him. His squad car was waiting at the corner. He helped me into the backseat and put Ribbons on my lap. Of course, she was up licking my face immediately.

Just as we started away from the curb, I noticed the pusher leaning up against a building. I guess he had been viewing from afar what had been going on in that alley. Should I tell the cop?

I decided I'd better live up to my deal. That pusher meant nothing to me, and Ribbons meant a lot to me.

"Officer, look over there on the left. See that guy leaning up against the building? He's wearing a black jacket. That's the pusher."

"You mean the guy in the black jacket and brown pants?"

"Yes, he's the one. He's the one who sold me the dope. He's the one who rented me those works."

"You did mean you'd work with us, didn't you?" the officer said over his shoulder. "That is Julius Cranshaw. I've busted that guy a couple of times, but I never have been able to get a court case against him. He's one of the smartest guys on the street. Whenever we bust him, we never find anything on him. We've heard he carries no more than two bags at a time."

"Maybe that's right, officer," I said. "That's what he sold me."

"One of these days I'm going to catch him with those two bags on him," the officer said. "That will be enough to put him away for a good, long time."

At the police station I was quickly booked and taken to a cell. They let Ribbons come with me; the cop had lived up to his end of the bargain. But what if I got sent to prison? No judge was going to let a girl take her dog with her to prison! Where would Ribbons go then?

Being in that cell was a horrible, degrading experience. It seemed so cold, so damp, and so utterly confining.

I was so exhausted and weak that I flopped onto the hard bunk. Ribbons jumped up beside me. After a few minutes, the stark realization of where I was hit me. I was so angry and frustrated by the turn of events that I walked over and began shaking the barred door. Ribbons seemed excited by the whole experience. She just slipped out under the door and started down the hallway. Every once in a while she'd turn and bark for me to follow her. When I didn't, she'd run back to me and bark some more.

"Ribbons, don't you understand?" I asked. "I can't come with you. I'm in jail. I've been a bad girl and I got caught."

Ribbons kept on barking, and before long the matron appeared. "You'll have to keep that dog quiet," she yelled, "or I can't let her stay with you. Don't you know we're doing you a favor? Now make her shut up!"

"Here, Ribbons," I called. "Come here, now." She walked through the bars and jumped into my arms as I leaned over to pick her up. I guess she knew she'd better be quiet.

I flopped onto the bunk again, and Ribbons was soon asleep. I tossed and turned, worrying about what was going to happen to me now.

The following morning the matron came to take me to a little room where a detective was waiting to talk to me. He motioned me to a chair. As soon as I sat there, Ribbons jumped into my lap. I couldn't help but wonder how much longer I would get to keep her.

"What's your name?" the officer asked.

I fleetingly thought of giving him a fake name, but I decided I was already in enough trouble. I'd better tell the truth. "Jackie Marshall," I said.

"The report says you're nineteen years old. Is that correct?"

Now I'd done it. I should have used an alias. They thought I was nineteen. That would mean I'd be treated as an adult. But since they had my real name, it wouldn't be long before they found out my true age. I'd better not lie.

"No, sir, I'm only sixteen."

"Sixteen?" he said in surprise. "But it says here you told Officer Krantz you were nineteen."

"I really didn't tell him I was nineteen," I replied. "Two men wanted to take me away in an ambulance, and they wouldn't let me take my dog with me. I had to tell them I was nineteen so they wouldn't force me to go in the ambulance and leave my dog behind. I couldn't leave my dog. She saved my life."

"I see," he said, rubbing his chin. "Yes, I heard about your dog. Well, that puts us in a whole new ball game. Since you're only sixteen, you'll be treated as a juvenile."

"Is that good or bad?"

He smiled. "In your case, it's probably good. Do you have a prior record?"

"No, sir. This is the first time I've ever been arrested."

"Good!" he responded. "Your being a juvenile and this being your first offense will work for you."

He asked my address and home telephone number. I told him the truth. I even admitted being a runaway when he asked me about that. I wasn't going to do anything to antagonize him or that might result in his taking Ribbons away from me.

"Okay, wait here for a few minutes," he said, as he shuffled the forms together. "I've got to check with a couple of people."

Moments later when he returned, he announced, "I called your parents. They're coming to pick you up."

"You didn't!" I moaned. "Why did you do that to me?"

"Regular procedure. I could go ahead and hold you in jail until someone bails you out. But since you're a juvenile I would have to take you to Spofford Hall. And I just couldn't see that as any place for a first-timer like you. I'd rather try to work this out and keep you out of jail. Jail's not going to help you any, and I couldn't let you take your dog up to Spofford."

Well, maybe my parents were the lesser of two evils. At least I stood a chance of keeping Ribbons with me.

"What will my parents have to do?" I asked.

"Well, I hope they'll take you home. And let me tell you, Miss Marshall, you'd better cooperate. Possession of a hypodermic needle is a very serious offense. The least little bit of static from you, and some judge will send you upstate!"

"You don't have to worry about me," I told him.

He smiled. "That's the way to go, Jackie. Sometimes I get teenage girls in here who are really mad at the world. I mean, they are just steaming with bitterness. Well, we have no choice but to put them away. They're dumb kids. If they would just cooperate with us, we'd help them work things out. But they just will not go home with their parents. So we have to put them away."

That really scared me. I didn't want to be sent to prison and be forever separated from Ribbons.

"I'll be taking you down to Officer Sterling," the detective said. "You can wait for your parents in her office. And don't get any funny ideas about taking off. If you try that and we catch you, you will be sent away. Do I make myself clear?"

"Crystal clear," I replied. "I'm not looking forward to meeting my parents, but I don't want to mess up anymore. I've got my dog to think about now."

The detective led me into another office and introduced me to the woman officer. "Have a seat, Miss Marshall," she said pleasantly.

"Her parents will be here to pick her up," the detective said.

When he left, I settled into a chair, and Ribbons jumped into my lap.

"My, what a cute little puppy," Officer Sterling said. "You're very fortunate to have such a fine dog. Where did you get her?"

Now I was in a jam. If I told her that a pimp had given me the dog, she would try to find out who my pimp was—maybe even hold me as a material witness. I didn't want to even get near Don Simpson again. So I lied: "My parents gave her to me for my sixteenth birthday."

"That's nice," she said. "I understand that you're not getting along too well with your parents."

"Ma'am," I said, "that is probably the understatement of the year. My dad's an alcoholic, and Mom is fast on her way to becoming one. They're both drunk half of the time and don't come home for days. I didn't know how to cope with that impossible situation, so I thought it would be best if I put some distance between them and me. I ran away, but didn't have anywhere to go and went back home. My dad beat the daylights out of me. I mean, I thought he was going to kill me. That's when I took Ribbons and split—for good."

She was taking a lot of notes, so I figured I might as well give her something to write down. Besides, if I laid it on thick, maybe she wouldn't get around to asking a lot of embarrassing questions, such as where I had been since I had run away from home.

"How come they found you with a needle in your arm?"

"Ma'am, with all the terrible things I have been through, I was depressed like you wouldn't believe. The only way I could be free from misery was to take drugs. I knew if I didn't take drugs, I wouldn't be able to cope, and I'd end up killing myself. So I guess you might say that by taking drugs I was saving my life."

A quick little smile flitted across her face. "Miss Marshall, you almost didn't save your life; you almost killed yourself. I understand that they picked you up as an overdose case."

I didn't like the direction her questions were taking, so I decided to change the subject. "Do you like being a police officer?" I asked.

"It has its ups and downs. If I can help people, it's very gratifying. But sometimes I get a young lady who tells me one lie after another. Then it's kind of hard not to get bitter and upset and chuck the whole thing."

She knew something was wrong, but I thought I'd still better keep her from asking so many questions. "Are you married?" I asked.

"Not yet, but I've got a man on the string. Do you have a boyfriend?"

"Yes, two of them. I can't make up my mind which one I like best," I lied. I went into a long description of them both, and she listened patiently.

Then we talked about where she had gone to school and whether it was difficult for a woman to be a police officer and get respect from the men officers—anything to keep up the conversation. We never did get back to where I had gotten Ribbons.

After what seemed like ages, someone knocked on the door. When Officer Sterling said, "Come in," the door opened, and there was the detective ushering my parents in.

One look spoke volumes. Mom's face was tearstained, and she looked terribly embarrassed. Dad's face was livid with rage.

I knew I was in for big trouble!

11

Mom looked as though she wanted to say something, but she just stood there, shifting uneasily and twisting a tissue. But words were no problem for my car-salesman father. "Jackie, where in the world have you been?" he demanded.

"I robbed a bank."

"You robbed a bank?" Dad roared. "Why in the world would you do something stupid like that?"

"Because I needed the money for drugs."

Dad gestured wildly at the policewoman. "Why didn't the officer tell me that when he called?" he shouted. "Why didn't he say something about her robbing a bank?"

Officer Sterling walked over to where they were standing. "Mr. Marshall, I think your daughter is just trying to act tough in front of you. She didn't rob a bank."

That aggravated Dad so much that, forgetting where he was, he started toward me. "I'll teach her what tough is," he shouted. "When I get through with her, she'll know I'm the one who's tough. And she'll never dare run away again!"

"Now, now. I think you'd better calm down, Mr. Marshall," Officer Sterling said, unobtrusively moving between Dad and me. "I know you're upset over this whole situation, and you're probably embarrassed about having to come here to the police station. Those are normal reactions. But frankly, this is no way to treat a daughter who has run away."

"I'll tell you how I'll treat her," Dad threatened, not losing an ounce of his belligerence. "I'll spank her rear end until she won't be able to sit down for a week. There's nothing wrong with her that a good spanking won't fix!"

"Jackie, would you mind stepping into this rear office, please?" Officer Sterling asked. "I need to have a private talk with your parents."

She opened a door behind her desk, and I walked into a small office. Ribbons trotted along after me. I wondered if I should cut out now. I knew my dad was going to beat the daylights out of me when he got me home.

Ribbons seemed totally unruffled by the turn of events and almost immediately went to sleep in my lap. I sat there twisting and turning, especially when I realized that the only way out of this office was the way I had come in!

I guess we sat there for at least half an hour. Every once in a while I could hear Dad yelling something, but I never could make out exactly what he was saying. Then Officer Sterling opened the door and said, "Okay, Jackie, you are free to go now."

The word *free* should have excited me. Sure, I had gotten free of a pimp. But was I really free? I just knew my dad would make me a virtual prisoner at home. He'd probably ground me for twenty years! Prison might be preferable!

My folks hadn't had anything to eat before they came to the station, so we stopped at a drive-in restaurant. Dad was the only one who ate much. None of us were doing any talking. I had heard people talk about a situation in which silence was deafening, and I lived through it and understood it on that drive home.

As soon as we got home, I started up the stairs to my room. I had almost lived a lifetime last night—the experiences with those two johns, escaping from my pimp, and then overdosing, and I was emotionally and physically exhausted. But before I had gone up three stairs, Dad yelled, "Jackie, come here!"

Both of them were standing at the bottom of the stairs looking as though I owed them an explanation. That was the last thing I felt like doing now.

"I think we'd better talk," Dad said.

Talk? I noticed both of his fists were doubled, so I stayed where I was and asked, "Are you going to beat me?"

"No, I'm not going to beat you. But if you don't get right down here, it'll be hard not to!"

I quickly came down the stairs, Ribbons at my heels, and followed my parents into the living room. I sank into a chair, and they sat together on the sofa.

"Jackie, don't you know that you have embarrassed your mother and me to death?" Dad started in. "Can you imagine what it's like to have to go down before breakfast and get your daughter out of jail? I mean, we both felt like criminals. I think it's horrible of you to put your poor mother through an ordeal like that. And I don't know what this is going to do to my business when the word gets around. You are the most selfish, inconsiderate, thoughtless. . . ."

I just stared down at the carpet, ignoring his tirade.

"Jackie, did you hear a word I just said?"

How could I help but hear him?

"Young lady, when I ask you a question, I expect an answer! Now, are you going to stop using drugs?"

I raised my head and looked at him blankly. "Who told you I was using drugs?"

"Now, Jackie," Mom said, "it's not necessary for us to

have a long conversation about all this. I'm sure you're exhausted, too. Officer Sterling told us everything that happened. She said you were nearly dead when they found you. I guess that dog of yours saved your life."

So that's why that policewoman had sent me out of the room. She had to rat to them everything I had done. I guess there was no sense in stonewalling it, now. They knew about what had happened.

"Well, uh, I guess I learned my lesson," I stammered. "I'm not going to do that again." I figured that by being vague I wasn't really promising anything except that I didn't plan to overdose again!

"Are you really going to quit?" Dad demanded. "I mean, do you promise never to take drugs again?"

I had to get him off my case. "Yes, Dad. I promise. Cross my heart and—"

"Don't get cute!" he ordered. "Now stay right here. I've got something to show you that will help guarantee that you'll behave yourself from now on!" He got up and walked back to his bedroom. I wasn't all that curious about his show-and-tell.

"Oh, Jackie, what you've done is terribly embarrassing," Mom told me. "I don't know how I'm going to be able to hold my head up in this neighborhood again. We've always tried to give you what you wanted. We've sacrificed for you so you could have things. And this is the way you've repaid us. Jackie, it's the most—"

That did it. "For crying out loud," I exploded. "All you two think about is yourselves. Don't you think it's time somebody thought about me? I've been gone for weeks, and you don't even act as though you've missed me. All you care about is that I embarrassed you because you had to come down to the police station. Don't you even care what's happened to me since I've been gone?"

"Yes, honey, I care," she answered softly. "I have

worried night and day about you. I haven't had a decent night's sleep since that night you left home. I've contacted the police and filled out endless forms. No one could find any trace of you. Where were you?"

"Mom, the very night I left home I was picked up by a pimp and held captive until I was able to escape last night. I had to run for my life! That's what happened to me!"

Mom gasped. "Do you mean to tell me that my little baby daughter was out working as a prostitute?"

"Well, not really. The pimp let me live in his apartment with him and the other girls until last night. That's when he started sending me out. But I used my brains and got out of all that filthy stuff. But I was held captive, and I did have to run for my life. He could easily have killed me. I could have been dumped in some filthy alley behind some garbage can and been another unknown. And you would never have heard from me again!"

Just then Dad walked back in. I looked at his hands to see what his great surprise was. Nothing!

Mom must not have heard all I told her, for immediately she said to Dad, "Do you know where Jackie has been? She's been working for a pimp!"

Before I had a chance to explain to him, he exploded. "A pimp? A dirty, rotten, filthy pimp? So now we not only have a drug addict sitting here in our living room but we also have a dirty, rotten, filthy prostitute! Jackie Marshall, you are the scum of the earth!"

"Don't you dare call me a prostitute!" I screamed back. "Don't call me scum. I fled for my life because I was held like a slave. I almost died in the process. Now I've come back home, hoping for a little love and sympathy. But I get nothing but the worst here." I was on my feet now, shaking my finger into his face. "Maybe I am scum," I shouted. "But you know what they say: Like father, like daughter!"

Whap! Dad's hand came down hard on my face as he yelled, "We are going to take you to a doctor. You're probably filled with filthy disease! How could you? How could you?"

By this time he was slapping me again and again. Poor little Ribbons leaped at him, grabbing his pants leg. He wheeled and kicked her clear across the room. She squealed as though she had been hurt badly.

As I ran across the room to pick her up and comfort her, I screamed, "If you kick that dog one more time, I'll kill you!"

Dad reached into his coat pocket and pulled out a revolver. "Don't shoot, Charles!" Mom screamed. "Don't shoot!"

"I ought to shoot her," he yelled back. "We'd all be better off if she were out of our lives forever. She's been nothing but trouble since before she was born. Now she's a dirty junkie and a filthy prostitute, and we're supposed to love her and forgive her and pretend that nothing ever happened. And that stinking dog. I know where that dog came from. I'll lay you ten to one that that dirty dog came from that pimp, didn't it?"

I held Ribbons tightly, shielding her from that monster. Of course Ribbons came from a pimp. But Ribbons had become my friend.

"This puppy might have come from a pimp, but she's not a pimp's dog," I retorted. "This dog is the only thing I have in life. She saved my life. She's a beautiful puppy, and she never hurt anybody who didn't deserve to be hurt."

Dad took careful aim at Ribbons. "I ought to pull this trigger and blast that mutt," he snarled.

That was more than I could take. I gently placed Ribbons on the floor. Then, as I stood up again, I lunged for his gun and took him completely by surprise. The gun tumbled out of his hand and onto the floor. We both dived for it, but he beat me to it. He rolled over onto his knees and pointed the gun right into my face. "I ought to kill you!" he said in disgust. "You filthy—"

Mom was sobbing. "Oh, God, what has happened to this family? We've become a bunch of raving maniacs!"

"Pull the trigger! Pull the trigger!" I taunted. "Go ahead! Blast my brains against the wall! I've got nothing to live for!"

The gun was inches from my face, and I watched his trigger finger twitch. Would he do it? Had I escaped death at the hands of a pimp and from an overdose, only to come home and die from a gunshot wound inflicted by my own father? At that point, I really didn't care.

Mom grabbed his arm and tried to pull the gun away. "Don't be foolish, Charles!" she screamed. "You'll go to the gas chamber for something like this!"

He brushed her away roughly. "Leave me alone, Nancy! I'm not through with this scum, yet!" He got up off his knees, and I edged my way back toward the wall where Ribbons lay whimpering.

"Jackie, I want you to take a good look at what I've got in my hand," Dad said in measured tones.

"I know what guns look like," I retorted.

"Now don't get smart! I want you to tell me now if you're going to go on being a dirty, stealing junkie and a disease-filled prostitute. Because if you are, I'm going to save everybody a lot of trouble. I'm going to kill you right now!"

Once again I found myself staring down the barrel of his revolver. The situation was absolutely preposterous. Deep inside of me something crumbled. Then the tears started.

Dad stood there, almost like a statue, with his gun pointed right at me. Mom had flung herself over the arm of the sofa, sobbing hysterically.

Maybe Dad was right. Maybe it would be best if I

were out of the way. I certainly had been nothing but trouble to myself and everybody else, lately.

"Go ahead, Dad. Pull the trigger. I'm no good. I'll never be any good. So blast me to kingdom come!"

He stood there, ashen faced. I screamed it again: "Pull the trigger! Pull the trigger! Put me out of my misery!"

Mom ran over and threw her arms around me. "Jackie, honey, we do love you," she sobbed. "I know it doesn't seem that way, but we do! We do!"

I threw my arms around her. "Mom, I know you love me," I replied. "But I just can't take this anymore. I just can't take it!"

I pushed her away, picked up my still-whimpering Ribbons, and headed for the stairway. The thought occurred to me that my dad might shoot me in the back, but I really didn't care. I figured he was bluffing, but I wasn't positive.

As I got to the top of the stairs, he yelled, "Don't you dare run away again, young lady, or you're in for trouble—and I mean, *deep* trouble!"

He didn't have to tell me I was in trouble. I knew that!

I slammed my bedroom door and threw myself on the bed. When I did, I felt my switchblade. I guess I was so weak when they brought me into the police station that they hadn't searched me. Can you imagine that? Well, I don't know how it happened, but I still had it!

I pulled it out and flipped it open. If Dad beat me again, so help me, I'd use it on him. But would I have enough nerve to kill my own dad?

I lay there for some hours, too exhausted to do anything else. But once when I stirred, I became aware that Ribbons was still whimpering. Poor thing! I had no idea how badly she was hurt. What could I do for her?

I began checking her to see whether she had any broken ribs. She didn't seem to flinch when I poked her. Hey, wait a minute! How long had it been since the poor puppy had had something to eat? One good thing about living at Don Simpson's apartment was that she'd always had plenty to eat—and on time!

"Come on, Ribbons," I said. "Let's go see if we can find something in the refrigerator for you."

I had left my switchblade lying on the bed, and just before I started downstairs, on impulse, I stuck it back inside my blouse.

I carried Ribbons downstairs as I tiptoed into the kitchen. I spotted three leftover hot dogs in the refrigerator and decided one of them would assuage her hunger until I could get her some puppy food.

I had bent down to break up a hot dog for her when I heard footsteps behind me. I looked up, and there stood Dad. Had he come to say he was sorry, or to hit me again?

"Jackie," he started in, "I'm all mixed up over this thing. Could you tell me why you're doing the things you're doing?"

I straightened up and faced him. I didn't know if I could ever forgive him for threatening to kill me. And I really hadn't analyzed, at that point, why I had acted as I had. I could have told him it was because he beat me, but I knew that was only a symptom, not the real problem.

"Dad, I don't know why. I just do what I do; that's all."

That started him off again. "You're still a smart-mouthed kid, aren't you?" he bellowed. "I asked you a question. Don't give me the runaround!"

"For crying out loud," I yelled back. "I was trying to give you an honest answer. I told you, I don't know!"

Whap! I tried to cover myself to prevent a follow-up blow. Ribbons snarled.

"Don't you ever hit me again!" I threatened. "It may

be the last thing you ever do!"

He ignored that and raised his hand. I wasn't going to stand for this. I reached into my blouse and pulled out the switchblade. I flicked it open and screamed, "I was told to use this against perverted old men. As far as I'm concerned, you're a maniac. So go ahead! Hit me again! But I'm warning you, if you hit me, I'll plunge this knife deep into your heart!"

Dad's eyes grew wide as he realized the situation had suddenly changed. He relaxed his fists and started backing away. I knew I had him.

Just as I was savoring my moment of triumph and power, he lunged for a kitchen drawer, jerked it open, and pulled out a butcher knife that looked about a foot long. "Okay, Jackie," he yelled. "You want to play knife games? Well, I can play at that one, too! You take a swipe at me, and I'll take this butcher knife and plunge it right through your heart!" His eyes seemed to flash fire as he added, "And then I'll turn it until your blood runs all over this kitchen floor!"

Ribbons was still growling. I sure hoped he didn't take a swipe at her. But she was keeping her distance from him. And that was something I decided I'd better do, too. I was no expert with a switchblade. All I planned to do was use it as a threat. I'd really gotten myself into a corner.

Mom heard the commotion and came running. She threw up her arms in horror and yelled, "What in the world is going on? Both of you nuts put those knives down, this instant! Do you hear me?"

"This daughter of yours needs to be taught a lesson!" Dad yelled back. "She thinks that just because she's a prostitute and has a switchblade, everybody's going to do just what she says. Well, no way am I knuckling under to some teenage thug like her!"

While Dad was making his explanation, Mom grabbed his wrist. "Drop that knife right now, Charles!" she ordered.

Dad tried to fight her, but she started twisting his arm, and the knife sailed across the floor. When Dad didn't make any effort to go after it, I clicked my switchblade back and stuck it into my pocket.

Ribbons took advantage of the lull in the storm to rush over and wolf down that hot dog. "I just came down to the kitchen to get my poor puppy something to eat," I said. "I didn't expect to run into a maniac down here."

As I stalked out of the kitchen, Ribbons at my heels, Dad screamed, "I should have left you to rot in that jail, you stinking, filthy, good-for-nothing, junkie prostitute!"

I was tempted to reach for my switchblade again. Instead, I just went back up to my bedroom. No sense hassling anymore today. A person could only take so much of this without breaking.

I knew I was exhausted when I woke up and realized I had slept straight through that day, that night, and until ten the next morning! When I went down for breakfast, Dad had already gone to work. That was good news. Mom didn't say much. She stayed out of my way. I could tell she didn't want to antagonize me.

For a whole week, I stayed around the house. Neither of my parents talked to me. I would have preferred that they yell and scream at me than ignore me! I felt as though I was losing my mind over it.

One evening as I was going out the front door to take Ribbons for a walk, Dad yelled, "Where are you going—out prostituting?"

That did it! I wanted to spin around and slash him. But I simply gritted my teeth and slammed the door behind me. I'd find a way to get even for that.

I walked and walked, wondering how I could get even.

When a police car drove by, I instinctively jumped back. But as it passed me, I got an idea.

I headed for our neighborhood police department, walked up to the desk, and said, "I want to report my father. He just raped me."

The sergeant looked up in surprise. "Your father did what?"

"He just raped me. He's a maniac."

The sergeant picked up his phone and dialed a number. "O'Malley," he said, "will you come here a minute? I've got one for you."

No sooner had he hung up than an officer appeared.

"O'Malley, could you take this young lady to your office?" the sergeant asked. "She's got something to tell you."

The officer led me into a small office, closed the door, and very gently asked, "Now, miss, what seems to be the problem?"

"Well, this evening my father came home drunk," I lied. "He said he wanted to talk to me in my bedroom. When we got up there, he closed the door and told me to take off my jeans. I protested, but he just laughed."

O'Malley sat there, expressionless, writing all this down. And I was enjoying the attention.

"Then what happened?" he asked softly.

"Well, I'm not about to pull off my jeans for any man. I'm a clean, decent, honest girl."

"Yes, I believe you," O'Malley said. "Go on."

"Well, when I didn't do as he said, he lunged at me and threw me on the bed and started ripping off my blouse and jeans."

I knew I'd better make this good, so I leaned my face into my hands and faked a good cry. When I did, even Ribbons started whimpering.

The officer came around his desk, put his arm gently around me, and soothed, "Now, now, little girl, everything is going to be okay. Sometimes these things happen in families. It's a horrible thing, and I know how you feel. But your father's probably a sick man. We'll look into this."

"Officer," I said through my sobs, "I'm afraid to go home. If my father finds out I've reported him, he'll probably try to kill me. Many times he's battered me mercilessly. But he's smart. He'll try to tell you I made all this up, and—"

"Well, we have the process of law to take care of it. But maybe we'd better call at your home. Is your mother there?"

"Yes, she is. But Dad will try to kill me if you go there."

"Don't worry. We'll protect you."

Officer O'Malley started out of the office. "What's going to happen now?" I asked.

"I'll get my partner, and we'll take you to the house. Let me ask some questions, and we'll take it from there."

In minutes, the three of us pulled up in front of my house. When I got out of the police car, Dad appeared in the doorway. "He'll go into a rage," I cautioned the officers. "And watch him. Sometimes he carries a gun!"

As the three of us reached the porch steps, Dad called out, "What did she do this time?"

"We've come to talk to you, Mr. Marshall," Officer O'Malley said. "May we come in?"

"Of course you can come in. But I'll tell you one thing; if she has gotten into trouble or stolen anything, or been into drugs, or whatever, you men can take her away and lock her up. I want nothing more to do with her!"

If he only knew why the police were there! This would be a moment I expected to relish for the rest of my life!

Once inside, Officer O'Malley explained, "Mr. Marshall, your daughter has filed charges of incest against you. She claims you raped her in her bedroom."

Dad's face turned to an expression of total shock as that soaked in. Then he lunged at me, screaming, "I'll kill that dirty—she's nothing but a prostitute and a junkie. And she's a filthy liar!"

I jumped back and yelled, "Watch him, officer. He may be armed!"

Before I knew what was happening, the two officers spun him around and kicked his feet out from under him. As he crashed to the floor, both of them pounced on him, and one of them handcuffed him. One of the officers searched him and found his gun. I should be so lucky!

"What's this, Mr. Marshall?"

"That's my gun!" he yelled. "Leave it alone! I'm going to use it to kill that little brat!"

That was all the officers needed to hear. They jerked him up off the floor and marched him out the front door to the squad car. Some of the neighbors had come out onto their porches when they saw the police car parked in front of the house. Now they got to see my dad, handcuffed, being marched before two officers and taken off to jail. I was at the height of my glory.

One of the officers returned and told my mother, "We'll have to book him on the complaint of his daughter and on carrying a concealed weapon. Do you know whether he has a permit for the gun?"

"No," Mom replied. "I know he doesn't. He said he didn't need one."

"He's wrong about that," the officer said. "You can't have a gun in the city without a permit." With that, he was gone.

Mom stood there on our front porch, watching the police car disappear in the distance, and not believing this strange turn of events. I figured she probably wanted to get rid of Dad, anyway. She had said he beat her and she was thinking about leaving him. Now I'd made that decision easier for her.

I put my arm around her and escorted her back inside. "Jackie, when did your father hurt you?" she asked.

"Mom," I lied, "it was about two years ago. I've held the whole situation inside me until tonight. I just couldn't take it from him any longer. I knew I had to get out from under his power. He's just a dirty old man."

The next day I had to go to the police station to sign a statement. They kept Dad in jail, but they said he could get out if someone posted bail.

Mom insisted that she had to do that. I tried to tell her not to. But a week later she announced to me that she'd finally been able to get enough money together and she was going down to bail him out.

That meant he'd be coming home! Now I was in for it! As soon as Mom left the house, I threw a few things into a suitcase, grabbed Ribbons, and left for the subway.

I knew better than to go back to Times Square, so I headed for Greenwich Village and Washington Square. I sat there on the square, wondering what to do next. Suddenly my thoughts were interrupted by a man's voice saying, "Hey, you good-looking thing. What's up?"

I stared. Ribbons snarled. Who was the handsome guy—another pimp?

12

Somehow the man seemed to fit into the Washington Square scene. Before I could answer his question, he had another one: "Hey, babe, want some pot, cocaine, LSD, uppers, downers, or the best heroin from Turkey?"

What luck! I was just barely off the subway, and in the middle of the day I had run into a drug pusher! After all I'd been through, it sure sounded like a great idea.

"How much for two bags?"

He did a little jig and answered, "Hey, babe, two bags? No problem. But maybe a little problem. Not a big problem; just a little problem."

From the strange way he was acting, I assumed he was high. But then I noticed his pupils weren't pinpointed. No, he wasn't high. But he sure was a doll!

"What's the problem?" I asked.

"I was hoping you would ask," he responded. "You see, I'm waiting for my shipment. I mean, it's a big shipment of dope. But it hasn't come in yet. So right now all I'm doing is taking orders. I'll put you down for two bags at fifteen bucks a bag—that is, if you pay me the thirty bucks now. But if you wait until my shipment comes in tonight to buy them, they'll be thirty dollars a bag. So you see, babe, you save one hundred percent by paying me now. Pretty good deal, huh?"

What was with this nut? Didn't I look as though I'd been around enough to see through that con game? He'd take my money, but that would be the last I'd ever see of him.

"Hey, Broadway dancer," I said, "I'm not just in from the country. I've lived in New York City all my life. No way!"

He burst out laughing. "Okay, Miss Smarty, I'll work another deal with you—one that will pay off immediately. Interested?"

"I'm always interested in hearing about deals."

"Okay. See that guy over there?" He pointed to a man in a business suit who was sitting on a park bench reading a newspaper. I nodded.

"Just a few minutes ago, he told me he wanted a girl. I mean, that guy really has got the money, and I know he'll pay big. He has wads of money stuffed in his pockets. Now I know I can get at least two hundred dollars for a young, good-looking chick like you. So the deal is that because I got the contact, you give me half the money. Okay?"

Prostitution had always turned me off. But I knew I was going to have to have some quick money to survive in this jungle, or some pimp would pick me up again. And it wouldn't be as though I were going to go into prostitution. It would just be this one time, until I could get a steady job.

"Okay, you're on," I said.

"Great!" he exclaimed, beaming. "Here's the key to my apartment. See that building over there?" He pointed. "It's 2-B. You can use it."

I studied the kid. Was he a pimp tempting me now and planning to use me later on? I sure didn't want to get into that kind of a mess again. But this kid looked so young and clean-cut—and probably naive. What I really planned to do was to go through with the deal and then cut out and keep the whole two hundred dollars.

I put on my most seductive smile and headed for the businessman. When I got right in front of him, I stopped. He didn't even look up. He sure didn't seem very anxious.

He was so lost in that newspaper that finally I said, "Hey, mister, want to have a good time?"

He looked over his paper and acted as though he wasn't sure what I had said. So I smiled beguilingly and purred, "Mister, I'm the most beautiful girl in New York City. Let's have a great time together!"

He stood up, folded his paper, grabbed my blouse, and jerked me up straight. "You filthy little prostitute," he started in. "What I ought to do is take you over my knee and spank you. Now get out of here before I call the cops!"

What was the matter? This sure wasn't the kind of response I had expected after what that kid had said.

"Hey, what's up?" I asked. "You don't sound interested."

"Of course I'm not interested!" he bellowed. "I teach here at the university, and I know you girls are full of disease. Now go!"

He released his grip, pushed me back, sat down, unfolded his newspaper, and began reading again as if nothing had happened. I stood there, nonplussed. When he glanced up and saw me still standing there, he yelled, "Get out of here now, or I'll call the cops!"

I spun around, shocked and embarrassed. Then I spotted that kid underneath a tree. Apparently he had been watching the whole deal, and now he was laughing so hard he was holding his sides. He knew something I didn't know. So I walked over and said, "Hey, you almost got me in big trouble."

He was laughing so hard he couldn't answer, and that made me furious. "Listen, creep!" I yelled. "What did you do to me, anyway?"

"Hey, come on. Can't you take a joke?" he asked.

"Who are you, anyway?" I asked.

"The name's Larry Childs," he replied. "I'm a student at the university."

"Then you're not a dope pusher?"

"No. I've never done dope in my life. I'm in the drama department at the university. One of our projects is to write a play visualizing life as it really exists. So when I saw you, I thought I'd play a little game. I mean, you've given me at least one hundred pages of fantastic material! I am indeed indebted to you."

I sure didn't think it was funny—a practical joke at my expense. "Listen, buster," I said, "I've never done anything like that before in my whole life. I rationalized that it would be a way to make some quick money, and I never planned to do it again—ever. And then to be embarrassed and called all sorts of names. I mean, what I ought to do is pull out my switchblade and rip out your guts so you'll never again be tempted to play what you call a joke on some poor girl!"

"Hey, come on. Calm down. I'm really sorry you got embarrassed over it. I didn't think about that."

His apology left me cold, so I spun on my heel and stalked to the other side of the park—anywhere to get away from him.

I began figuring out my options as I sat down on a bench. What was I going to do? How was I going to support myself? Where was I going to live? I started looking through my purse to see what I had brought, when suddenly I spotted it—the key to that kid's apartment. He had given me his key, and he'd forgotten to get it back. Here was a way to avenge myself and also teach him a lesson. Besides, I should get something to hock for spending money.

I looked around the park and spotted him going in the direction of his apartment. I'd go over there later, when he wasn't around.

Just as it was getting dark, I headed for the apartment building. It was quite nice outside. The kid must have a lot of money to live in a place like this.

I quickly found 2-B and listened intently at the door. Was he home? Was he asleep? I decided the only way to find out was to knock. If he answered the door, I'd take off.

I knocked and then put my ear to the door. No sound. Good! But just to be sure, I knocked again. Then a voice behind me almost made me jump out of my skin: "I don't think he's home."

I spun around to see an older man dressed in a business suit. "Oh, thanks," I said. "I thought he'd be back by now. Do you know Larry?"

"Yes. He's a student. I know his parents, too. They're really talented people. Larry's just like them. They've shared their wealth with him, and he's never let it go to his head. He's really an all-around great boy. They're a beautiful family."

I was already seeing dollar signs and drooling to get inside of that apartment. But I couldn't let this guy see me going in there.

"Well, if you see him, tell him Sylvia Porter called," I said, and started down the hall.

I walked out to the street, but the man followed me. That was making me a little uneasy. But when we came to a corner, I went one way and he went another. Just a coincidence, I thought, that he had followed me out.

When the man was out of my sight, I dashed back to Larry's apartment. I knocked again—still no answer. So

I whipped out the key, turned it in the lock, and slowly opened the door a crack. I peered inside. No one seemed to be around. I stepped in, closed the door, and flipped on a light. Wow! Talk about a plush apartment. It looked like a pimp's apartment because it was so expensively furnished. But I guessed that was because his folks had money.

He probably had money laying around, too, and maybe jewels. I searched a couple of dresser drawers but found nothing but underwear, socks, and shirts. But in the nightstand I hit pay dirt. I found a stack of bills that I quickly estimated to be about two hundred dollars. That went into my jeans immediately. Then I almost jumped out of my skin again when a voice behind me asked, "And just what do you think you're doing?"

I spun around, and there stood Larry Childs!

I bolted toward the door, but he stuck out his foot, and I unceremoniously flopped onto the floor. He pounced on me like a tiger, grabbed one arm, and twisted it behind my back. "You came to rob me, didn't you?" he asked in disgust.

"No, no!" I said. "You have it all wrong. I just came to explore your apartment. After all, you gave me the key. Besides, I'm still embarrassed and upset over what you did to me. I've about decided to report you to the police!"

"Report me to the police? Ha! I saw you take my money out of the nightstand." He reached into my pocket and pulled out the two hundred dollars. "I ought to report *you* to the police, you thief!"

"That's a great idea, Larry," I said. "You go ahead and call them. Because as soon as they get here, I'll accuse you of being a pimp. And you're going to do time for that. I mean, big time. I'll get that professor to testify that I propositioned him. And then I'm going to point the finger at you. You'll go to prison for that, buster. I'll get fifteen days for prostitution. But you may get fifteen years!"

He didn't say a word, but I felt him relax his grip and get off me. I rolled over and looked up at him. He was ashen faced.

"Really? I could be busted as a pimp?"

Naive! This guy sure hadn't been around! And he was supposed to be writing about life as it really exists?

"You'd better believe you could!" I declared, laying it on thick. "These New York City cops are tough on pimps. I know what it's all about."

"You do? Who are you, anyway?" He extended his hand to help me up and motioned me to a chair. "Let's talk this out."

I sank into his plush sofa. It felt good to relax.

"Are you really a prostitute?"

I felt so embarrassed. Evidently this was a good kid, and I felt so dirty when he said *prostitute.* I sure didn't want him to get the wrong idea about me.

"Well, yes and no," I told him. "A pimp held me prisoner and tried to use me that way, but I got out of it. I nearly got killed, though. When I went back home, my dad beat me up again. So, Larry, I'll level with you. I'm a runaway."

"A runaway? In my apartment? Can you imagine that?"

"Well, that's what I am."

He laughed easily. "This is getting better and better. I can do my whole script around you. What other exciting things can you tell me?"

"Well, for starters," I said, "what do you know about pimps?"

"Pimps?" He leaned forward eagerly. "That would be great! A dramatic play about pimps. That would go on Broadway!"

I told him about my life with Don Simpson. He sat

there spellbound, so I really poured it on. He kept asking details: Where did I go, how much did I charge? Did he want to get into the business?

When I got through telling him how I escaped and how I overdosed and then went home, he moved over onto the sofa and put his arm around me. He really seemed concerned.

"Do you know you've been telling me all these intimate details of your life," he said, "and I don't even know your name?"

"I'm Jackie Marshall."

"Hey, I like that name! Glad to meet you, Jackie Marshall."

He stuck out his hand, and I grabbed it. But before I knew what was happening, he threw his arms around me and hugged me.

"Jackie," he said, "when I first saw you, I really liked you. Now don't get me wrong. I come from a good family, and I have no devious thoughts in my mind. But I think you'd make a fantastic sister. Can I be your big brother?"

I don't know why, but I grabbed him and said, "Hi, brother."

"Hi, sis," he replied. "But I'm going to call you Jackie because I really like that name. Okay?"

I nodded. Then he said, "I'll bet you're starved. Why don't we go out and get something to eat?"

"Great idea. I am hungry."

When I stood up, it hit me! I'd forgotten all about Ribbons! I yelled, "Oh, no! My dog! I forgot all about my dog!"

I started toward the apartment door, but Larry grabbed me and spun me around. "I've got a little surprise for you," he said.

He led me out to the kitchen, and there was Ribbons happily gnawing on a bone.

"What? How? Where?" I sputtered.

"Well," he said, "she came over to me when you took off this afternoon. I figured if she didn't mean any more than that to you, I'd keep her."

"Oh, no," I said. "You can't do that. She saved my life!"

"I know, I know," he responded. "So I guess because I got my two hundred dollars back from you, I'd better not try to steal your dog!"

This was fun. Larry had quite a sense of humor.

Ribbons came over and started jumping on both of us. Larry must be okay because Ribbons sure liked him.

He picked her up and told her, "Ribbons, you be a good girl and stay here while I take Jackie out to dinner. Okay?"

Had Ribbons and I found a home? But what was I going to have to pay for it? What would Larry expect of me in return?

We had a lovely steak dinner at a beautiful restaurant with wonderful atmosphere—candles, flowers, the works. It was really romantic. Larry paid in cash. He did have money.

We went back to the apartment and talked some more. Then I told him, "Well, I guess I'd better be going."

"Going? Where are you going?"

"I don't know. Just going, I guess."

I held my breath. Would he invite me to stay?

"Hey," he said. "I think you're forgetting something. You agreed to be my little sister. I wouldn't think of letting my little sister leave at this time of the night. This is where you live now. This is your home."

I threw my arms around him and said, "I thought you'd never ask."

Next I knew he was going to suggest I sleep in his bed. How was I going to handle that one?

"You can sleep in my bed," Larry suggested.

Well, there it was. But what could I say? I had nowhere else to go, but could I get by with some excuse?

Larry must have been reading my mind. "Whoa! Whoa!" he said. "Remember, you're my little sister. You can sleep in my bed, but I'm not sleeping in there with you! I'll sleep here on the sofa. It opens into a comfortable bed."

Whew! That was close!

The arrangement worked very well for a few weeks. But one Saturday night we went out for dinner, and we both drank—and drank too much. By the time we got home, we were both very drunk. And we drank some more when we got home. Well, we lost control over our emotions, and Larry spent the night in my room. After that, he never moved back to the living room.

At first I felt rather dirty, but I got over it because Larry was very good to me, and we always had enough and to spare. His parents gave him one thousand dollars a month spending money, so we lived high together for a number of months.

Larry studied hard and kept his grades up. I did the cooking and the housekeeping. The two of us were now deeply in love, and I began to think about marriage.

I never did tell my parents where I was. I figured it was best if I were completely out of their lives.

One night—a night I'll never forget—I had supper all ready for Larry at the usual time. But he didn't come home. I got nervous. There was no telling what could have happened to him. Did he get mugged? Had he been in an accident?

When eight o'clock passed and he still wasn't home, I really got frantic! I didn't know what to do, but I felt as though I ought to be doing something, so I grabbed Ribbons and went out into the park. I sure felt nervous being out there with all the pushers, addicts, pimps, and prostitutes. I'd been clean ever since I'd moved in with Larry. I had too many good things going for me to foul them up with drugs.

Ribbons and I walked all the way around the park, but never did see Larry. What in the world could have happened to him?

When we went back to the apartment, I looked at the lovely meal I had fixed. It was just sitting there, and I sure didn't feel like eating. I was furious at him one minute, for not calling and telling me he would be late. And the next minute I was terrified that something had happened to him. Even Ribbons wouldn't eat. I guess she could sense how I felt.

I watched the eleven o'clock news, hoping maybe there would be some clue on it—maybe a disaster, or a subway crash, or something. But there had been no disaster in New York City that day.

Suddenly I heard steps in the hallway. Our door opened, and there stood Larry. I started to remonstrate about his being so late when I had dinner waiting. But one look told me that something was dreadfully wrong.

I threw my arms around him and asked, "Honey, where have you been? I've been so worried."

When he didn't say a word, I drew back. Then I noticed his eyes. His pupils were pinpointed! Larry was high!

13

"Larry, what have you been doing?" I yelled, knowing full well the answer before I even asked the question.

He didn't even try to explain. He shoved me aside and headed for the living room, grumbling "Where's my supper?"

This certainly wasn't the Larry I knew and loved.

I figured I'd try to make the best of it and not upset him, so I answered, "It's still on the stove. Just a minute, honey, and I'll heat it up for you."

As I scurried around the kitchen, I worried about what I was now almost certain of: Larry was on drugs. I peeked into the living room and saw him nodding and scratching, just like a junkie!

When I called him into the kitchen to eat, he just sat down and started in. Still no explanation or even, "I'm sorry I'm late." Nothing. From across the table I sat there staring at him, not believing what I was seeing. No longer was I looking into the eyes of my lover; I was now looking into the eyes of a junkie!

"What you staring at?" Larry demanded.

"Oh, I was just thinking what a hunk of man you are," I lied. "You always look so handsome."

That was about the extent of the conversation during the meal. I cleaned up the kitchen after he had finished eating and hurried into the living room, where Larry had gone, still nodding and scratching.

He looked up and smiled. "I really got some good stuff this time," he volunteered. "Makes you feel good, doesn't it?"

He never should have said that. Ever since I'd been here I'd stayed clean, and I thought I had made up my mind to keep it that way. But when he reached into his pocket and pulled out a bag, asking "Want some?" I flew off the sofa and snatched that bag out of his hand. The temptation was irresistible.

"Where are your works?" I asked.

"In the bathroom."

"In the bathroom? How long have they been there?"

"About two months." He smiled like a little kid who has been keeping a big secret.

"Two months?" I responded incredulously. "Do you mean to tell me you've been getting off for the last two months?"

"Yeah, man. I'd get off just before I left for school. Then I'd sit in the park for about an hour and just nod. That's how I prepared myself to face school."

I just couldn't believe it! For the last two months I had had a junkie in my house, and I didn't even know it! I wondered if Larry were already hooked. If he were, there was big trouble ahead. But right now the excitement of being able to get off again far overshadowed any little worries about what might happen if Larry were hooked.

I found his works taped underneath the toilet bowl, pulled them out, and laid them on the counter. He even had his cooker there.

I loaded up and drilled myself, and did I ever take off! I went sky high! Whatever Larry was getting, he sure had a tremendous connection!

I put the works back where I had found them and

walked back to the living room. Sitting there next to Larry, I was in another world.

The following morning I got up when Larry did. Just before he left for school, we got off together.

That night we got off again. The next morning we got off. The following night we got off. And so it went, day after day, night after night.

Of course, about a month later we had to start increasing our dosage or we couldn't get high. Our bodies were building up immunity against the drugs, so we needed more bags.

In the back of my mind, I knew our drugs must be costing Larry a bundle of money. Was he getting more money from his folks?

I finally got the answer to that one night. I knew things were getting tight because Larry hadn't given me any money for groceries. The refrigerator was getting more and more bare. The cupboards were getting emptier and emptier. And that night, after we both had gotten off, Larry said, "Jackie, I don't know how to tell you this, but I spent my last forty dollars on dope. What we just shot was all I had left. There's nothing else."

"What?" I yelled. "You did what?"

"I told you, Jackie, this is the end of the road. I have no more money. I have no more dope. The rent is three months behind, and the landlord is threatening to kick us out. And there's no food—not even for Ribbons!"

"Larry, we've got to have money," I moaned. "Don't you know what's going to happen in the morning? I mean, if we don't get off in the morning, we are going to get sick. And I do mean sick! We're both going to be vomiting all over this place, wishing we were dead!"

"Hey, I'm smart enough to know what's going to happen," he replied. "We've got to figure something out, quickly!"

Why hadn't the stupid guy shared the problem with

me before we got to this stage of desperation? I could have been out looking for work or something. But Larry hadn't wanted me to take a job. He liked me to be there and have his meals waiting for him when he came home. After all, he had plenty of money from his folks. His folks! Hey, that was it!

"Larry, can't you just call your folks and say you need some more money this month?"

"Are you kidding?" he responded. "I did that last month. I don't know whether you know it or not, Jackie, but we have been shooting up over two thousand dollars a month in dope! I asked my folks for extra money last month—told them I was making some investments in Wall Street. I don't think they believed me, but they sent the money. But I can't go back again. They're likely to find out what we're doing, and they'll cut me off completely. They have no use for dopers!"

"Well," I said, "that leaves only one other choice. We're going to have to go out on the streets and start mugging people. Are you up to that, Larry?"

"For crying out loud, Jackie, I could never do anything like that! I come from a good family! I couldn't rob or steal. Besides, if we did that and got caught, we'd do five to ten years. You know this city is tough on muggers. I mean, no mercy whatever!"

Larry was right. We both sat there staring at the floor. What could we possibly do?

Without ever looking at me, Larry finally said, "Why don't you go out tonight and make some money?"

"What do you mean by that?"

"Well, you told me you used to work for a pimp. I figured you'd know what I meant."

I jumped off the sofa and shook my finger in his face. "Listen, Larry, there's one thing I'm not going to do no matter how sick I get. I'm not going to go out and prostitute! No way! Not for you or for anybody else! I don't see how you can claim to love me and even suggest such a dirty, filthy thing!"

"But Jackie," he protested, "what are we going to do? If we mug somebody, we could get fifteen years. If you get caught prostituting, it's only fifteen days. I'm just thinking about you. I don't want you put away for fifteen years. Do you want to go to prison for fifteen years? You know, fifteen days we could live with. I could even be there to bail you out, and—"

"That's what you say," I interrupted, enraged. "Sure, you can sit there and think up all these great ideas that don't cost you anything. But what about my self-respect and decency? Absolutely no way!"

"Okay," he said, with a shrug of his shoulders. "Let's go out in the street and see what we can do. I don't know one thing about knives and guns. You're going to have to teach me."

"Well, the first thing we've got to do is get a gun," I said. "I can't teach you anything about them until we get one."

"Jackie, Jackie!" he cried, burying his head in my lap. "Tell me this is a horrible nightmare. I can't believe I would do anything so evil as to stick a gun in somebody's ribs. I can't believe it!"

"You think that's horrible, do you?" I said, pushing him back into a sitting position. "How horrible do you think it is, getting into bed with some pervert? Some of those guys will pull a knife on a girl and cut her body up into little pieces. Other screwballs will try to offer her as a sacrifice to their guilt. You think that's nothing compared to fifteen years in prison? And you try to tell me it's against your principles to mug somebody? Come off it."

"Jackie, Jackie, can't you see? If we get caught and my parents find out about this, it's all over for me!" He was on his feet now, shouting and gesturing wildly.

"Will you stop shouting at me?" I shouted. "Both of us are in this together. We got a little too greedy and kept shooting up too much. Now we're hooked. We've got to get some money. And I say the best way to do that is with a gun. So we've got to go out and get a gun."

He threw himself back down on the sofa, protesting, "But don't you understand, Jackie? The gravy train is gone. I don't have a penny to my name. Where are we going to get the money to buy a gun?" He buried his head in his hands. "I hate myself for even suggesting it. I can't stand the idea of you with another man. But Jackie, it's the only way I can think of. If you'll do it just this once, we'll use the money you make to get a gun. That will be the end of the prostituting. I promise."

"Never!" I answered. "I've still got my switchblade. We'll try that first."

I headed for the closet where I kept my switchblade in the toe of a shoe, dropped the knife into my blouse, and Larry and I headed for the street.

"Where do we start?" he asked.

"Let's try Houston Street," I suggested. "And let's hope that whoever we pick has got some money!"

I was trembling all over as we walked down Houston Street. Never in my wildest imagination would I have dreamed that I would stoop to something like this! Suppose we got caught? I couldn't live through fifteen years in the penitentiary!

Ahead of us, we spotted an old lady waddling along. "Larry," I whispered, "let's go for her. You come up behind her and slap your hand over her mouth. I'll flick my switchblade open in front of her face. You talk right into her ear and tell her if she makes one false move, it's all over for her. Then grab her purse and run for all you're worth."

"Suppose this doesn't work?" Larry asked. "It doesn't look as though she's got any money."

"Stop making stupid comments," I said. "I don't know whether she's rich or poor. It's hard to tell by looking. Besides, we've got to start somewhere!"

Larry didn't respond, but I could see him nervously cracking his knuckles.

When we started toward the old lady, she glanced around at us and then quickened her pace. I'm sure she knew what was up.

Suddenly Larry leaped forward, grabbed her from behind, and slapped his hand over her mouth before she had a chance to scream. I flicked the switchblade open right in front of her nose, and her eyes bugged. She looked as though she could have died of fright right on the spot.

We didn't have to say anything. She extended her purse toward me. I grabbed it and took off. Larry spun the poor old lady around and threw her to the ground. I heard her moan. I felt so sorry for her, and so ashamed of what we had done.

Larry quickly caught up with me, and we ran for about three blocks, then turned into an alley where we ripped open her purse, pulled out her wallet, and found twenty dollars. Rats! No wonder she hadn't put up a struggle. That wasn't enough to do anything with. Throwing the purse and wallet into a nearby garbage can, we took off.

Larry wanted to go back to Houston Street. "Don't be stupid," I told him. "That area will be swarming with cops by now." So we headed for Twenty-third Street.

We picked out another old lady and went into action. Larry slapped his hand over her mouth, and I flicked the switchblade open in her face, the same as before.

But this old lady wasn't so docile. She swung around

to hit me with her purse, and began to kick wildly. Then her wig flew off, and out of nowhere cops appeared from every direction. Oh, no! We had tried to mug a decoy cop!

I darted across the street. Cars screeched to a halt trying to avoid me. Larry was smart enough to split. He took off the other way.

As quickly as I could, I turned down a darkened alley and slumped behind a garbage can. I heard footsteps, but they passed right by where I was.

By this time, I was completely out of breath and scared to death. But so far I had been lucky. Was Larry that lucky?

I hunched there in that smelly garbage for what seemed an eternity. Finally, I eased out and looked around. Nobody. I tiptoed to the end of the alley and turned a corner to where I could see out onto the street. Oh, no! Just down the street was a police car with two cops inside. They had staked out the alley! They must have suspected I was in there!

I spun around and hurried to the other end of the alley. As I peered around that corner, I spotted another police car. They had blocked me in! How was I going to get out of this?

I figured I'd better head back to my hiding place. It was darkest there. In case they decided to come back through there, I could duck back down.

I slipped back to my spot and just happened to look up. Right above my head was a fire escape. Maybe if I could get up on the roof, I could keep an eye on those cops.

I jumped several times before I finally caught the lowest rung on the escape ladder. Then, putting my feet against the building, I pulled myself up, rung by rung. It took all the strength I had, but I was desperate.

When I finally got my feet onto the fire escape, it was easier. From there, I quickly made my way clear to the top and out onto the flat roof.

I walked toward the street and looked down, careful to keep out of sight. Sure enough, the police car was still there, waiting. Same thing on the other side.

As I headed back toward the middle of the roof to see if I could think my way out of this predicament, I stumbled slightly on an old brick lying there. A light went on in my mind. If I could throw that brick through a window across the street, it might set off a burglar alarm. That would distract those cops!

Again I went to the side and peered down. What luck! Right across the street was a jewelry store. It would have an alarm!

But the question was, did I have enough strength to throw the brick that far? And was my aim good enough to hit a window?

I couldn't see much point in wondering. I had to try.

I grabbed the brick tightly, strained to get as much power as possible behind it, aimed, and heaved it as hard as I could. It sailed toward the street. Oh, no! What if it hit somebody who was passing by and killed him? I'd go to prison for life!

I watched the brick and realized it was going to miss the mark. It was veering too much to the left. I had been lucky to find that brick. It would almost be a miracle if I found another.

I had just turned around when I heard *crash!* I peered over the side of the building and realized I had hit something, because everything broke loose. Sirens started screaming. I hadn't hit the window of the jewelry store, but I had hit the glass door.

I waited. From both sides of the building, two police cars raced up, lights flashing, sirens blaring. It had worked!

I knew that even if they discovered it was a ruse, they would still have to stand guard until the door was boarded up, or somebody would be right there, helping themselves to all that jewelry! So I quickly hurried back to the fire escape and down to the alley. This time, when I got to the street and peered around the corner, the way was clear. No police car!

I circled far to the left for several blocks, and then on down to the Village. The apartment door was still locked. "Larry?" I called as I entered. But only Ribbons came to greet me. Had Larry been busted?

I waited all that night. Still no Larry.

In the morning the nausea hit me. I had to make some money now. I couldn't take this. And when Ribbons started to whine for breakfast and there was nothing to feed her, I knew what I had to do. It was the last option.

I put on my tightest outfit. I had said I would never do this, but it was this or kick cold turkey. I couldn't face that. Already the pain in my stomach almost made me pass out.

I headed for Forty-second Street, walked up to a guy, and asked, "Want to have a good time?"

He smiled. "Sure. Why not?"

I went with him to his room. I'd hit the lowest point in my life. I had become two things that I had said I'd never, never become. I was a junkie and a prostitute!

When we got through, I located a pusher and bought some drugs. I even rented a set of works from him so I wouldn't have to go back to the apartment.

I also knew that one time wasn't the end of it. I had to buy food for Ribbons and me. I had to make some money to pay the rent. I still needed a place to stay.

So I spent the rest of that day prostituting. On the way back to the apartment, I bought a few groceries and some dog food. Poor Ribbons was sure happy to see me—and the dog food. The poor thing had been starving all day while I had been gone.

But there was still no sign of Larry. I had some drugs, and I got off by myself. That way I wouldn't have to think about what I knew I was going to have to do tomorrow and the day after that and the day after that. . . .

14

One day sort of melted into another. My whole life revolved around prostituting to get money and getting high to forget I was prostituting.

But one night when I walked into the apartment and to my bedroom, I was almost startled to death! Someone was in my bed! Had some pervert broken in? Was he waiting to jump me?

When I screamed, the man threw back the covers. There was Larry!

"What are you doing here?" I yelled, running over and hugging him.

"Those cops caught me and busted me, but my parents finally agreed to get me out on bail," he explained. "At first they weren't going to do it. They said I could rot there, as far as they were concerned. Dad said he had no use for a junkie. But I guess Mom finally talked him into putting up the bail."

He looked at the way I was dressed and asked, "What have you been doing?"

What was I going to tell him? Oh, well, he probably had guessed it, so I might as well tell the truth. "I've been working on Forty-second Street," I told him, trying to avoid his eyes. "The Times Square area."

He didn't react at all. He just asked, "Got any dope?"

"Yes. Do you want some?"

He sprang out of that bed. "Man, do I ever! I had to kick cold turkey in that filthy jail, and it was horrible! I mean, horrible! Man, I need to get off. And I mean, get off now!"

I pulled two bags from my purse and handed them to Larry, and he headed for the bathroom.

We sat around talking. He described in detail his experiences in jail. It was sickening.

The following evening, Larry went with me to Forty-second Street. He started to make contacts outside the nicer hotels. I always got more money from the men who stayed there.

For about three months, I made lots of money, but we were shooting it all up as soon as I made it. I hadn't gotten busted yet, but that was an ever-present possibility.

About ten o'clock one night, I was standing on Forty-second and Eighth looking for a trick when a woman walked up to me. "Here," she said, trying to push a little booklet into my hands, "this is something you might be interested in."

I eyed her suspiciously.

"My husband and I have a wonderful place for you in Garrison, New York," she went on.

"What do you mean, a place for me in Garrison?" I asked in surprise. "You don't even know me. Who do you think I am, anyway?" I figured I'd better watch my step with her. She might be some kind of a nut.

Worse than that, she could be a plainclothes cop! I started backing away.

"Please," she said, "it's not necessary for you to be defensive. My husband and I have been caring for girls like you for many years now. God has burdened our hearts to come here to Forty- second Street and tell you about Jesus."

"Jesus?" I echoed. "What are you—religious fanatics?"

She laughed easily. "Some people think we are. But there's really only one reason we're out here. It's that Jesus has a beautiful life planned for you, and it's not here on the streets, using drugs and hustling."

I started to protest that I was neither a hustler nor an addict when a nicely dressed man walked up. "This is my husband, the Reverend John Benton," the woman said.

I stared at him. He looked honest enough. But was he a cop?

"And I'm Mrs. Benton," she went on. "The girls call me Mom B."

I started to acknowledge the introduction, but before I could say one word, she had stepped toward me, slipped her arm around me, and hugged me!

"You'd make us a wonderful daughter!" she exclaimed. "You're so cute!"

What did she mean by that? I'd already gone that daughter route with Don Simpson, and I sure didn't want that again!

Before I could protest that I didn't want to be anyone's daughter, she kissed me on the cheek!

I drew back in surprise. "What in the world are you up to?" I asked. "You don't even know me, and you're hugging and kissing me. What's your game?"

Mr. Benton stuck out another brochure. "It's no game," he said. "God has given us a beautiful place upstate in Garrison, and we use it to help girls who have problems. And we're both for real."

I took the brochure and started thumbing through it. It showed a beautiful mansion, and lots of girls. The girls who were pictured had such happy faces. They must have been able to get it all together somehow. They were probably kids from loving, happy families spending a summer in the country.

I handed the brochure back and said, "Sorry, folks,

but this isn't for me. I'm hopeless."

I turned to walk away, but they followed. Somehow I had to get rid of them so I could get back to work. We needed the money. And I wasn't sure I could trust them.

"Listen, people," I said, turning toward them, "I don't know you, and you don't know me. I've got work to do, so I don't have time for things like this."

Both of them looked so hurt, almost as though I had slapped them in the face! Maybe they were for real.

"Listen," Mr. Benton said, "maybe you don't need any help right now. But someday you might. Please take this pamphlet. It's called *A Positive Cure for Drug Addiction.* Our address and phone number are on the back. Call us when you need us."

"Oh, thank you," I said, "but I don't need that kind of help. I'm okay." But I still took the pamphlet.

From across the street, Larry caught my eye with a signal that meant he had a customer for me. I didn't even tell the Bentons good-bye. But as I crossed the street, I ripped the address and phone number off the pamphlet, tucked it into my blouse, and threw the rest of the pamphlet away. *A positive cure for drug addiction?* I thought. *Those two must be living in a dream world!*

When I walked up, Larry took me aside and whispered, "Why didn't you turn a trick with that guy?"

"Are you kidding?" I laughed. "That was a minister with his wife. They run a girls' home in upstate New York and claim they can help me."

Now it was Larry's turn to laugh. "Listen, baby. I've never heard of girls like you getting help. I mean, the only help you can get is from me. Understand?"

I nodded. I knew there was no way out for either of us. We were too far gone. We'd probably die as junkies.

"Okay, you stop wasting time talking to do-gooders," Larry warned. "You've got to keep busy. Now I've got a guy set up." He nodded toward a man who was standing nearby. "He's ready to go."

I left Larry, walked over to the guy, and said, "Follow me."

We walked two blocks to the run-down hotel I was using. The clerk at the desk only charged me three dollars whenever I used a room.

When we got up to the room, I closed the door and said, "Okay, business before pleasure."

"How much?"

"For you," I said, looking him over, "it'll be fifty bucks."

I held out my hand for the money. He reached into his coat pocket and flipped out a badge!

"You're under arrest," he said. "Don't try anything funny!"

I bolted for the door, but he spun me around and slapped his handcuffs on me in one, smooth, practiced motion. Then he pulled his gun. Keeping it aimed at me, he said, "You must think I'm kidding! This is for real!"

He pulled out a little card and read me my rights. I didn't say a word, but I was thinking about Larry. How stupid could that idiot get—setting me up with a plainclothes cop! Now I was headed for jail!

The detective grabbed my elbow and led me downstairs. People stared at us. I felt so degraded, so dirty—and so helpless!

Another cop was waiting out on the street. He said he'd already called for a squad car. A few minutes later, when it arrived, they unceremoniously pushed me into the backseat and headed for the nearby police station.

Still handcuffed, I was marched inside and up to the front desk. They asked me a lot of questions and warned me not to make any false statements, or they could charge me with that, too. I decided to tell the truth, except about my age.

"You have one phone call," the sergeant at the desk told me. "Whom do you want to call? Your lawyer? Your parents? Your pimp?"

I wanted to slug his smart mouth, but I knew I needed to make this phone call count. Call my parents? They wouldn't care. Larry? He couldn't bail me out. He'd already spent that night's earnings on dope. Wasn't there anybody who could help me?

Then I remembered that minister and his wife I had just met on the street. They had said to call when I needed help. Well, I sure needed help right now. It was a good thing I had kept their address and phone number! I pulled the piece of paper out of my blouse and poked it at the sergeant. "These people might help me," I said. "Can I call them?"

"Hey, lady, you have one phone call, the law says. You can call the moon if you want. Call anybody. It's your dime!"

He led me to an office where I dialed the number. It seemed an eternity before I finally heard, "The Walter Hoving Home."

"Hi, you don't know me," I said. "I'm Jackie Marshall. I've just been busted down here in New York City. Can you people help me?"

There was a pause. Then the girl said, "We sure can. Where are you?"

"At the police station on Fifty-fourth Street."

Then she told me that the Bentons usually visited the girls in the jails. As soon as I heard that name, it rang a bell. "Oh, you mean the reverend and his wife? I just met them out on the street not long ago."

"Hey, that's right," the girl responded. "They often go out on the streets at night telling people about the new life that Jesus has to offer them. You're fortunate to have met them."

She could say that again. At least there was a ray of

hope streaming into my darkness.

"It will probably be tomorrow morning before Mrs. Benton can get there," the girl said. "Will that be okay?"

Of course, I was hoping she'd come right away. But tomorrow was better than nothing, so I merely said, "Yes, that'll be okay. And thanks."

The police took a mug shot and booked me for prostitution. Then they took me to a cell where I was to spend the rest of the night.

That had to be one of the longest nights I've ever experienced. The bunk was too hard to sleep on. All kinds of strange noises wakened me every time I started to doze.

After breakfast the next morning I had a visitor—Mrs. Benton. She walked in with that same big smile on her face. Of course, she hugged and kissed me. Then she held me at arm's length and looked at me closely. "Say," she said, "I remember you. You're the girl my husband and I talked to on Forty-second Street last night, aren't you?"

"Yes," I responded. "And I told you I didn't need help. Well, right after that, I got busted."

"That might be all for the best," she reassured me. "You see, if you hadn't gotten busted, you wouldn't have called us. I'm glad you're giving us a chance. How can we help you?"

"Well, I don't know," I replied. "I really didn't know who to call, but I took a chance and called your place. You see, I propositioned a cop. That means they'll throw the book at me."

"I'm sorry to hear that," she said. "And I'm really sorry that you're here now, Jackie. But no matter how low we go, God's got a long reach. He can still reach us."

She smiled again, and I got the feeling that whatever happened, she was on my side.

"Let's sit down," she suggested. "Maybe you could

tell me a little bit about yourself."

I began with the problems I was having at home. And about the drugs. And running away. And the pimp. And Larry. I just let it all out. I even mentioned something about Ribbons, and when I did, I suddenly worried about what was going to become of her now.

"No problem," Mrs. Benton said. "I can go to your apartment and check on your poodle. Besides, maybe Larry's still there, and I could see Larry, too. We have a boys' program called Teen Challenge. Wouldn't it be wonderful if the Lord made it possible for Larry to go to Teen Challenge and you to come to our home?"

"You mean you have homes for both boys and girls?"

"We sure do. And God has done such wonderful things in both programs. We've helped people who were into drugs, alcohol, crime, prostitution—all sorts of problems. It's remarkable what God has been able to do in their lives!"

She sounded so hopeful. But I knew I'd still have to face the judge, and probably a jail sentence.

As we talked, she began to tell me about Jesus. He seemed so far away from me, but she talked as though He was right there with us. I really couldn't understand it. But she said He loved me. When she prayed for me, something strange came over me. I learned later it was love—Christ's love. All I knew then was that I broke down and started to sob. And Mrs. Benton cried along with me. I'd never known love like that before.

After she left, I was taken downtown to be arraigned. I was scared to death, as I went before that judge. I knew I was going to be put away, and I sure couldn't take that.

But as I stood there before the judge, I happened to glance around, and who do you think was there? Mrs. Benton! She really was interested in what was going to happen to me!

The judge asked me how I wanted to plead. There was

no sense trying to fake this one. They had me. So I said, "Guilty, your honor."

"Well, then, Jackie Marshall," the judge said, "since you plead guilty, I'd like to give you a choice. You can either go to jail or to the Walter Hoving Home."

I looked up at him in surprise and wonder. Then I turned and glanced at Mrs. Benton. She was all smiles.

"The Bentons are friends of this court," the judge went on. "I know they have helped many girls. Since this is your first offense, I can give you a break. Now what do you want to do?"

"Oh, your honor, I'd like to go to the Walter Hoving Home."

"Your wish is granted," he said, pounding his gavel on the bench.

I spun around and saw Mrs. Benton heading for me, arms extended. I knew what was coming next—another hug and a kiss!

I was taken to an office where we had to fill out some probation reports. The judge wanted to see me again in six months.

I walked outside to freedom, and Mrs. Benton drove me to the Village so I could pick up my things at the apartment. Reverend Benton had already gone back to the home. Mom Benton told me she had been working on my case and that she and her husband had decided I could keep Ribbons with me in Garrison.

Larry was at the apartment. I told him all that had happened, and Mrs. Benton began to talk to him about Jesus and Teen Challenge. Larry was ready for anything that offered hope, so we both packed.

Mrs. Benton drove us first to Teen Challenge in Brooklyn, where we dropped Larry off. He seemed nervous, but he said he was willing to try anything to get clean.

Then Mrs. Benton and I headed upstate to Garrison.

When we drove onto those grounds, I couldn't believe the beauty of that place! *Gorgeous* is really inadequate to describe it. And immaculate, too. But beyond that, there was a peace and love about that place that I'd never experienced before. The girls there were all so friendly and helpful. I learned later that many of them had been in even more hopeless situations than I had been in.

Ribbons loved the place and the attention. She became everybody's dog and really thrived on all the activity.

Mrs. Benton introduced me to the other staff members, and then one of the girls took me on a quick tour of the place. I couldn't get over its beauty. She told me it was made possible by gifts from Christians all over the country—Christians who loved and wanted to help girls like us.

When we got back from the tour, Mrs. Benton wanted to see me in her office. There she asked me if I wanted to receive Jesus as my Saviour. I told her I really didn't know what she meant. So she asked me if I was a sinner.

I looked at her in surprise. "Of course," I answered. "I've done some pretty disgusting, dirty things."

She next explained that my sins—big ones or little ones—would send me to hell. But Jesus loved me so much that He came to earth and died on the cross. He took my place and died so that I could be forgiven of all my sins, if I would just ask Him to do it.

That sounded great, but what she told me next almost blew my mind: "Not only will Jesus forgive your sins," she said, "but He will also pour His love into your life and make you a new creation!"

I sat there hungrily drinking it all in. I just had to have what she had—and what these girls had!

She explained that I had to do only three things:

1. I was to acknowledge that I was a sinner. No problem there.

2. I was to ask Jesus to forgive my sins. She showed me from the Bible that He had promised that if I asked Him, He would graciously forgive me.

3. By faith I was to receive Jesus into my heart and life.

Then she had me repeat a prayer after her, and I shall never forget it: "Lord Jesus, I confess I am a sinner. Please forgive all my sins and come into my heart. I receive You by faith now."

After I repeated the prayer, she asked, "Jackie, where is Jesus now?"

I thought, and then I remembered what I had just prayed. "I asked Him to come into my heart," I said. "You told me He would do that if I asked Him; so I'd say He's in my heart!"

She got up and came over and hugged me. "That's right, Jackie. That's exactly where He is right now. And He'll always be there, as long as you want Him to be there."

As I sat there thinking about it, I suddenly began to feel warm all over! Christ's love began hitting me like a huge waterfall. It was so beautiful, so uplifting. I knew something great had happened. I felt such peace, and I felt clean inside. I had been saved, born again! I was a new creature in Christ Jesus!

I went through the one-year program at the Walter Hoving Home. Sure, I had my ups and downs. But Jesus was always there to help me. I learned to grow in Him from our studies in the Bible.

During that time, I prayed for my mom and dad. I wished there were some way I could share with them the love and forgiveness I had found through Jesus. Finally, I found enough courage to contact them. To my surprise, they wanted to visit me. I was nervous about the meeting, but I agreed to see them.

Imagine my joy when I discovered that my parents,

too, had been born again. They had prayed and wept over me, wondering where I was—and whether I was even alive! We became a loving family again.

I kept in contact with Larry. He was doing well at the Teen Challenge center and eventually went to the boys' farm in Rehrersburg, Pennsylvania. He also had been born again!

We both graduated from the programs. I studied hard and was able to take a high-school equivalency test. And then both of us, feeling God's call upon our lives, headed for the same Bible school: Valley Forge Christian College in Phoenixville, Pennsylvania.

For four years we studied there together. And we dated. I thought I had been in love with Larry before. But now I knew for sure that I wanted to spend the rest of my life with him. I'll admit it was hard to wait, but we both agreed that we should give ourselves to our studies while we were in college and wait to get married until after graduation. And we did. Graduation was on Saturday. We were married on Sunday!

That was two years ago, and Larry and I are happier and more in love than ever. We don't have any children yet, but Ribbons—well, she's another story. Ribbons had four puppies, each one as cute and lovable as she.

Thanks for listening to my story. I have prayed that as you read it you would understand the absolute folly of the kind of life I was living and that you would come to know my Saviour, too.

Maybe you're looking for peace. I never found it at home or on the streets. I found it at the Walter Hoving Home. But it wasn't the home. I found peace in Jesus. So wherever you are, Jesus wants to give you peace and freedom, too.

Let me tell you something else: It isn't difficult to receive forgiveness for your sins. Why don't you do what I did in Mom Benton's office? You know you're a sinner. I don't have to convince you of that. Step two is to ask Jesus to forgive your sins. No, you don't have to name them one by one. Just say, "Jesus, please forgive all my sins. I'm sorry for them."

The third step is to receive Jesus into your heart by faith. You may not feel different immediately, but the feelings aren't the most important part. As someone once said, "Faith first, then feelings." Just believe Jesus will do what He said. That's faith.

All of this can be summed up in a beautiful verse from the Bible. Maybe you've heard it: "For God so loved the world, that he gave his only begotten Son, that whosoever believeth in him should not perish, but have everlasting life." It's found in John 3:16.

Do it right now. You don't know what tomorrow might bring. I pray that right now you will receive Jesus as your Saviour.

Larry and I are living proof that it works. We were as low as any two people could get. But Jesus loved us and saved us from our sins. Now we're busy telling others about His great love—a love you've never known before! Jesus is exactly what *you* need!

The Walter Hoving Home.

Real people — Real problems —

New Hope Books are drawn from John Benton's experience as director of The Walter Hoving Home for delinquent teenagers. The characters in these books have found new hope for their lives — hope that is available for all.

Look for New Hope Books at your local bookstore today.

Marji. A young woman who has everything leaves it behind to start a ghetto ministry. Can she survive in her new world? $2.50

Marji and the Kidnap Plot. An underworld scheme threatens to compromise Marji's ministry and endangers her life. $2.50

Marji and the Gangland Wars. Marji's determination to stop a gangland war puts her right in the middle, with no one to trust but her Lord. $2.50

SPIRE BOOKS
OLD TAPPAN NEW JERSEY